Turning Back Time

A Crestfield Inn Romance

Elsie Davis

Sweet Romance Publishing

Sweet Romance Publishing

Sweetromancepublishing.com

PO Box 778

Liberty, NC 27298

TURNING BACK TIME

Many thanks to all my readers.
May love and laughter light your path always...

John 8:32

And you will know the truth, and the truth will set you free.

Chapter One

♥

WELCOME TO CEDAR GROVE. *Population 5,154.* The green sign announced Sarah's arrival before the brisk male voice of the GPS resonated through her Mustang's speakers. The trip had been short and easy thanks to the Lake Champlain ferry and excellent weather. The crossing from Plattsburgh, New York to Grand Isle, Vermont took fifteen minutes, but it shaved off close to an hour of added driving through the winding, back-country roads.

Lucky for her, the groundhog got it right this year—no shadow. The end of winter was always a welcome relief after months of bitter cold and snow. Winter was beautiful, but best enjoyed by a fire with a cozy book and a glass of wine.

The unseasonably warm temperatures had melted most of the normally still frozen lake, and the journey had been smooth—although out on the open water, the bone-chilling frigid wind kept her in her car. Vehicles had been parked on the ferry like colorful sardines, but not a single person had braved the elements.

The ride from the ferry dock to Cedar Grove had taken her through several quaint towns, each one a unique part of the Green Mountain State. The towns she loved the most had sidewalks that connected the people as one cohesive unit, where evening strolls and riding bikes were common occurrences. A place where neighbors were either family or long-time friends. From the drugstore on the corner, to the diner on main street, or like the old church where she used to play bingo—history echoed from the rooftops, reminding all who lived in each of these towns or villages why the place they called home was special.

And Cedar Grove, it seemed, was one of those towns. There were historic homes that had been remodeled, businesses in the downtown district, a couple of streetlights, and sidewalks to connect it all together. *Quaint.*

She followed the GPS directions and found the Crestfield Inn smack dab in the middle of town and within walking distance to everything, just like the website claimed.

The new owner had recently reopened the French Colonial style mansion, and as luck would have it, she'd been able to book a room without much difficulty. Staying at the inn allowed her the luxury of becoming immersed in the setting for her double mission—that of finding out what really happened the night Captain Tremont, her great-grandfather six times removed, died, and scoring the research material for her next mystery novel.

Finding the telegram in her grandmother's long ago locked away antique chest had instigated the trip. It couldn't have come at a better time. In between stories was always the worst for Sarah. It was when she felt the most alone and cut off from the world. By choice, perhaps, but still alone. Anonymity was best served by seclusion that kept well-meaning people from constantly interrupting her ebb and flow or from figuring out her pen name. It also made it easier to avoid men and relationships, something she'd learned from experience robbed her of her creativity. The emotional drain always took a toll on her writing, her last breakup especially painful and a reminder she'd been a fool to break her no-dating rule.

Grabbing her purse off the front passenger seat, she tossed her phone in it and snatched up the reservation confirmation. She headed up the steps, pausing for a moment to look around before she walked through the open front door which she closed behind her out of habit. The scent of fresh roses in bloom filled the air, welcoming her.

"Welcome to Crestfield Inn. You must be Sarah Dalton." A nice-looking, friendly man, probably in his early twenties, spoke from behind the registration desk.

Her boots clunked against the hardwood floors as she crossed the room to check in.

"Yes. I've brought my confirmation if you need it." She pushed the paper across the desk and glanced around. Antiques added an aura to the room that filled one with a sense of history and days gone by. She spotted a dish of potpourri on the foyer table, identifying the source of the mystical rose scent lingering in the room.

"No need. I've got you right here. My name is Kyle. I hope you had a pleasant journey." The sincerity in his voice prompted her to answer with more than an automatic response.

"I did, thank you. I took the ferry from New York, and although the water wasn't too choppy, the breeze kept me in my car. We aren't quite as warm as I would like just yet."

Kyle typed a few things into the computer and within seconds the printer spit out a few pages. He placed them on the desk, turning them around for her to see.

"True. No matter how warm it is outside this time of year, the lake effect will have you bundled like you're in Alaska—but it is such an enjoyable way to travel. You're in room four on the second floor, to the right at the top of the stairs. It's a lovely room overlooking the gardens."

"Sounds perfect."

"And here's your key." He pushed a black metal skeleton key across the desk toward her.

"Nice touch. I didn't know they made locks that would work with keys like this anymore." This beat a city hotel any day of the week.

"They were a special order. When Jason Montpelier inherited the inn, he ramped up the remodeling, and he favors keeping the place authentic." The pride in his voice spoke volumes. It would seem the owner had found the perfect gate keeper.

"Wonderful. I can't wait to check it all out." She'd given herself this evening to explore the town before diving into her research at the courthouse tomorrow.

"We'll be full in a few weeks with the annual Maple Festival, but right now there's only a handful of other guests. The inn is three stories, and the main media room, if you need an internet connection, is right over there. There's also a small desk on each floor for workspace without internet." Kyle pointed behind her to the room on the right she'd passed when she first came through the door.

"Breakfast and lunch are served until two in the Garden Delight Bistro down the hall." He pointed toward the back of the house. "Jason serves a fantastic homemade breakfast that's simply to die for and it's open to guests staying at the inn. Be sure to try the chef's special jam. And for dinner, the restaurant is open Thursday to Sunday. Best to make a reservation though, as the place fills up fast."

"Is it too late to make a reservation for this evening?"

"I'm sorry, but I think so. Give me a sec and I'll check. Here's some information on Cedar Grove that will make it easier for you to find what you need. If you need any help or suggestions, come to me." His happy smile was contagious, and Sarah felt right at home.

"Thank you. I expect to be busy while I'm here, but if I need anything, I'll be sure to ask." Busy was an understatement. She had her work cut out for her and only five days to finish before she was due back home to start her next novel. Schedules ran her life on a tight leash.

"What brings you to Cedar Grove?"

"Research. I was cleaning out my grandmother's attic and found a note written to a man by the name of Captain Tremont back in 1815. The note mentions the Crestfield Inn and I'm trying to figure out who sent it and why."

Kyle's eyes lit up "*Ohhh,* I love a good who-done-it."

As did she—the mystery writer in her thirsting for the truth and her next story. There was no way she could have tucked the slip of paper back between the pages to leave it for another two hundred years. The captain would make an excellent main character, whether villain or hero hadn't been decided.

"Jason might be a good one to ask for help. He inherited the place from Bettina Crestfield. She shared a lot of stories with him as they were quite close, and there's a ton of stuff still locked away in the attic. Seems the people who have owned the inn in the past were like pack rats. I'm sure there are records boxed up somewhere."

"Great idea. I'm headed to the courthouse in the morning to research some of the old records while they're open. Perhaps after that, I'll seek out Mr. Montpelier."

"Good thinking. As to dinner reservations for this evening, we are booked. You could try Bixby's Diner, Murphy's, or Cades Tavern. They all serve food.

Sarah stacked all the papers together, placing the map of the town on top. "Thanks. I'm sure I'll find something, and it'll give me a chance to check out the Cedar Grove. I'll just get my suitcase and settle in." She headed for the door while glancing down, trying to make heads or tails of the drawing.

She pushed the door open with her shoulder. It slammed into a solid wall—well, more like a man carrying a box judging by the expletive he uttered as the box rocked and a lamp fell off the top and crashed to the ground.

Sarah winced, reaching for the lamp. "I'm sorry. I glanced down at the map for two seconds and didn't expect anyone to be coming in." The base hung at an odd angle, broken away from the post.

The man peered from around the side, a hard expression on his face. He set the carton down on the porch and held out his hand.

She went to shake it, realizing too late all he wanted was his lamp. Embarrassed, she pulled her hand back and shoved the lamp toward him instead. "It's broken. I'm sorry." She shot the man an apologetic look. Her first real impression of him was impressive, given the not-so-impressive meeting.

"*Great.*" The sarcasm lacing the single word spoke a greater truth about how he felt. Apparently, *he* wasn't prone to accidents. "One less antique for Jason to find a home for."

If it weren't for the sour face, she would have thought him an attractive man. Thick chestnut hair, cut short, and with waves like the ripple of water currents, had been brushed to one side, the style setting off his angular jaw. It was a perfect complement to the dark-framed, geeky glasses magnifying brown eyes that remind her of dark chocolate. Early thirties, perhaps, and in excellent shape, his broad shoulders and chest emphasized by the tight T-shirt he wore.

"*Antique?*" She winced. "Again, I'm sorry. Maybe there's something I can do to fix it?"

"Maybe, maybe not. Not your concern, but perhaps you could watch where you're going, for everyone else's sake." He scowled, dropping the lamp in the box with a clang.

It's not like she'd run into him on purpose, and his rudeness was fast becoming a bore.

"What's going on? Is there a problem?" A tall man joined them on the porch, a concerned frown on his face as he looked from her to the not-so-happy man standing protectively near his precious cargo.

"Nope. No problem, Jason. The lady ran into me at the expense of one of the antiques I was bringing you, but otherwise all good."

Jason. The owner of the inn. Just great.

"That's unfortunate, but accidents do happen. And after running this inn, nothing surprises me." The man's easy laugh made her feel much better.

"Mr. Montpelier?" She turned to the newcomer and held out her hand, determined to ignore the other boorish man and his pile of heirlooms.

"Call me Jason." He clasped her hand in his larger one, his warm and friendly greeting an echo of Kyle's earlier reception.

"Jason it is then. I'm terribly sorry about the lamp."

"Don't worry, honest. There's no shortage of old stuff around here, and we'll see what we can do to fix it. This by the way, is Blake Carter, our history teacher at Rushton High." Jason nodded toward the other man.

"I'm afraid I didn't make a good first impression with the teacher."

"Don't let him worry you none. He loves everything and anything that relates to the olden days, especially antiques. He's been instrumental in helping me find great artifacts for the inn, and as soon as I turn him loose in my attic to start cataloguing what's up there, he'll forget all about this incident. The place is the equivalent of a goldmine to a history buff." Jason shook his head and laughed.

"I'm standing right here and can speak for myself. I've already told the lady it was fine." Antique man had the good graces to look apologetic.

"In a roundabout sort of way." Sarah laughed, not afraid to call him out. He'd been rude and deserved the set down.

"I apologize. It's been a long day after dealing with sixty unruly teenagers who aren't into history. And yes, accidents do happen." Antique man held out his hand as an olive branch.

"Sarah Dalton." She accepted, his grip strong, and very masculine like. "It's been nice meeting you, but I need to go. Have a nice evening."

"Likewise." Blake nodded.

"Oh, and Jason, I'd like to talk to you later tonight or tomorrow if you have a few minutes. Kyle mentioned you might be able to help me with a project I'm working on." Sarah didn't want to miss a single opportunity to further her research.

A young couple came up the stairs, laughing and holding hands.

Sarah and the men stepped to the side, out of the doorway, to allow them to pass.

"Good afternoon. How was the hiking?" Jason greeted the couple, his voice warm and friendly.

"It was awesome. We had a picnic lunch down by the river. Thanks for telling us about it," the young woman answered, a look of adoration on her face as she glanced at her boyfriend. They waved, disappearing inside as the door closed behind them.

They were young and in love. Something Sarah wrote about, but so far, hadn't experienced. Not that she was looking.

Jason turned back to her. "Sorry, but to answer your question—absolutely. If there's anything I can do to help, I'm game." The inn owner's graciousness was no more than Sarah expected, having grown up in a small town where people went out of their way to be friendly.

"Thanks. I appreciate your help."

"Just let Kyle know when you want to talk. He always knows how to find me."

"Gotcha." She waved and headed down the stairs to her car.

As she opened the back-passenger door, she couldn't resist a glance at the two attractive men on the porch. What she hadn't expected to find, however, was them watching her. Embarrassed to have been caught looking, she turned away to grab a few other items.

It had not been an auspicious beginning to her stay, but it wasn't entirely her fault. Blake should have carried a smaller box if he couldn't see where he was going, at least to her way of thinking. Sarah finished gathering her bags and went inside, grateful the men had moved away and satisfied no one else was in sight.

She followed Kyle's directions and headed up the stairs, one hand gliding up the smooth wood bannister. Old photographs and paintings hung on the wall and scone lights illuminated her path. If the walls could speak, she'd quickly learn a great deal of history. Instead, she planned to explore every inch of the mansion, positive it would provide her with rich detail for her next novel.

Turning right at the top of the stairs, she found room number four. The door stood wide open, something you'd never see in the city, but it was another one of the small ways the place made her feel warm and welcome.

She gazed around, taking in the details. The oversized oak dresser and matching headboard appeared to be incredibly old and handcrafted, the spiral vines etched deeply into the wood. Gold brocade curtains framed the high window, the color complementing the patterned wallpaper and braided rugs. The queen size bed had a quilted cover, one Sarah was sure to be hand-stitched, and from a time when quality had been more important than quantity.

It was like she'd stepped back into the 1700s and all that was missing was her favorite gown and a dashing gentleman to accompany her to a ball. She laughed at her fanciful notion born of reading too many regency novels.

Sarah moved to stand in front of the window, peering out over the gardens and backyard. An odd sensation trickled down her spine, and it felt as though someone were watching from behind. She spun around, but no one was there. There hadn't even been a sound, just a feeling. A wave of cool air washed over her skin, causing goosebumps to form as she shivered.

The dampness had probably come from the window—old houses were notorious for drafts. She moved to close the door, turning the lock for peace of mind. It was one thing to have an empty room left open, quite another once she occupied it. This was, after all, the 21st century.

Chloe sensed a strong aura enter the house and it immediately intrigued her. She left the attic and floated down the stairs, wondering what could have provoked the rush of anticipation coursing

through her ghostly soul. A woman stood at the front desk, checking in. The closer she got, the stronger the pull grew.

Hovering off to the side, she watched and listened. Some people were more gifted when it came to the spiritual world and she didn't want to tip the woman off to her presence. Not yet anyway. There had to be a reason the woman's presence had the power to call out to her. Captain Tremont. The words drifted her way. Words she hadn't heard in over two hundred years. She moved closer, determined not to miss a thing.

A warmth she hadn't felt since she died washed over her—until that is, she remembered the rest of the story. The chilling truth of the past, and her part in it, filled Chloe with a deep-seated need to help this Sarah woman discover what really happened the night Captain Tremont died.

After Sarah gathered her belongings and returned inside, Chloe followed at a safe distance. The young woman made her way up the stairs to room number four.

Her old room. Chloe smiled. It was a sign destiny was at work.

Hanging back, she watched Sarah unpack and then cross to the window. Chloe couldn't resist a closer look. There was a striking resemblance to the captain. The girl's long, wavy brunette hair, blue eyes, and dark eyebrows appeared like a mirrored reflection of his face. She could still see the dashing officer like it were yesterday, waltzing around the ballroom floor, resplendent in his naval uniform. Chloe let out a deep sigh.

Always the watcher, never the dancer.

Except once.

Sarah tensed and turned, looking toward the door.

Chloe had been right to worry the woman might sense her presence. She'd leave for now because the last thing she wanted to do was frighten her away. Sarah would soon go to dinner and that's when she'd make her move. There was much work to be done and the courthouse was a waste of time. After two hundred years of waiting, Chloe felt entitled to a few subtle pushes in the right direction

waiting, Chloe felt entitled to a few subtle pushes in the right direction

Chapter Two

♥

FRIDAY MORNING AND A teacher's work-day—the perfect combination in Blake's mind. Normally, the day was to catch up on grading tests and papers, but he tried to never get behind for this exact reason. A day off.

He walked the two blocks from his apartment building to Bixby's Diner, whistling the whole way. The bells on the door chimed as he entered and found a place at the counter to sit. "Good morning, Katrina."

Full of early morning smiles, the owner waved hello as she rang up another customer. "The usual?" The woman was a master of multi-tasking, and her memory unlike anyone else he knew. She once boasted that she knew every customer who visited the café on a regular basis, what they liked and how they liked it.

"Of course." One extra-large bold coffee to send his brain into mental overdrive and an old-fashioned donut to ward off his hunger.

Standard breakfast fare to help him prepare for the challenges of students who would prefer to be anywhere other than in school. "On second thought, make that two donuts. I'm headed to the library and you never know when I'll resurface." He winked, although they both knew his comment came closer to reality than he liked to believe.

"You should take one of my quiches, fresh from the oven." Katrina was known for her top-secret recipes, ones that had been handed down through generations, and her baked goods—well, they were out of this world.

"I think Perry would frown on me bringing a meal into his sanctuary of books, but thanks anyway."

"Gotcha. Mind you take your head out of the books long enough to find your way here for lunch. Today's special is Shrimp Macaroni and Cheese." She stuffed a couple of napkins in the bag and handed it to him.

"*Hmmm.* Sounds great. At some point my stomach will demand attention and I'll be here. See you later." He adjusted the briefcase strap over his shoulder, freeing his hands to juggle the coffee and donuts as he walked to the library.

He passed several people along the way, waving hello to some, calling a greeting out to others. Friday had a way of bringing more smiles than any other day of the week, except from maybe the parents of the kids stuck at home on a teacher workday.

Blake arrived at the library a few minutes after eight, surprised to see Perry, the head librarian, unlocking the front door.

Mr. Punctuality, he opened exactly at eight and closed exactly at four. A stickler for the rules, he took his position seriously, to the point of driving everyone insane. No one dared turn in a book late on Perry Templeton's watch.

Blake walked up the steps to the library. "Either you're running a little behind or my watch is running a little ahead." He grinned at his friend, walking past him as he held the door open.

Perry was older by a few years, and another one of Cedar Grove's bachelors. In a town this size, the men tended to stick together against matchmaking mamas.

"Must be your watch." Perry shot him a glance that dared him to contradict. They both knew otherwise, but it wasn't up to Blake to play library police.

Perry flipped on the lights closest to the door and made his way around the main room to turn on all the other lights, illuminating the place with the soft glow of life.

Rows and rows of shelving held thousands of books, all categorized, and waiting for someone to take them off the shelf to investigate the secrets held between their covers.

Blake took a deep breath, never growing tired of the musty smell of old books. There was a ton of history housed inside these four walls and as a child, there had been nothing better than curling up in one of the reading nooks with a book. It was one of the main reasons he'd fallen in love with history. The more he read, the more he wanted to know—a cycle he'd never managed to break, even as an adult.

"Still researching the family tree, huh? What year you at now?" Perry moved behind the desk in the center of the room and flipped on his computer.

"Yes. I'm back to 1850 in the Gazette, but the microfilms are hard to read and it's slow going."

"You've been working on this project for over a year. Your mother didn't do you any favors giving you that DNA test kit. You know, living in the past won't help you much in today's world."

"Maybe it won't help me, but it's less stressful." Blake loved the Christmas gift, but his school schedule hadn't left much library time, which is exactly where he needed to be for access to the microfilm and reader. "Speaking of today's world, how'd your date go with Meredith last week?"

"It didn't. She cancelled." Perry shrugged.

"And that just proves my point. Besides, most women find history boring. Nowadays, going to a museum is like the kiss of death on a first date."

"Then maybe you should take them to the museum on the second or third date." Perry shook his head and laughed.

His love for history was common knowledge, but his determination to fill in the missing links on his family tree went far beyond antiques and museums and information on the local area—this was about people. His family.

He'd discovered generations of Carter relatives who'd grown up in Cedar Grove or in nearby towns and villages—and with each link he found a story. Fascinating accounts of people's lives were connected on a far more personal level than any other type of history he'd studied in the past.

"Maybe you're right. In the meantime, you can let me know how the dating game works out for you." Blake picked up his coffee cup and headed for the media room.

He laid his briefcase down on the conference table and made his way to the filing cabinet. After scanning through the folders, he pulled the files he needed and sat down at one of the microfilm readers. He switched on the lamp of the archaic monstrosity and loaded the first sheet of film.

He opened his notebook to the last entry he'd gotten from the courthouse records. *Matthew Lawrence married Holly Smith. July*

8th, 1868. The document had been water-stained and hard to decipher, but after hours of studying it, Blake was certain he had the date right. The link narrowed his search and with any luck, it wouldn't take him long to find Matthew's parents.

It had been a lucky find since the couple lived over in Bellevue, a town about thirty miles away and the town where Blake's mother lived. Matthew had originally been from Cedar Grove, which explained the mention of his marriage in the Gazette, but unfortunately, no other useful information had been listed on the entry.

Blake pulled the file starting with the year 1850. Assuming Matthew was at least eighteen when he married, it was a good place to start to look for his birth announcement. It didn't take long to realize some weeks and months had been missed altogether. War and challenging times had left their mark on people and businesses alike, but he hoped the missing pages didn't have the information he wanted.

Scanning through page after page, week after week, he kept moving the sheet into place. He squinted, trying to make out the words. His shoulders ached from staying hunched over the machine. Blake sat back and stretched, rubbing his neck to work out the tight kinks. He removed his glasses, rubbing his eyes and blinking several times.

The newspaper stories were interesting, and he couldn't help but stop and read some of them, always on the lookout for any mention of the Lawrence family. But it was the society page he was most interested in, the place where births, deaths, and marriages were to be found. Blake heard someone enter the room, the soft padding of shoes across the hardwood floor reaching his ears about the same time as the sweet fragrance of lavender. He sat up straight and turned, surprised to see the woman from the Crestfield Inn.

Sarah Dalton.

She glanced his way and did a double take when she recognized him. With a faint smile and half wave, she acknowledged his presence before looking away. He watched her place her things at the opposite end of the table and scan the room.

"Hey there. Fancy meeting you here. I thought you were on vacation. This isn't one of the most likely places to find someone trying to explore Cedar Grove."

Her gaze landed back on him. "It is if you're here to research some of the town's history." The word *history* was like gold dust to a gold miner.

"Is this how you normally spend your vacations?" He felt compelled to ask, considering yesterday, he wasn't sure she liked antiques, much less anything to do with chronicles of the past.

"I don't take many. Or at least, I haven't in a while." She shrugged as if vacations meant nothing to her. To him, they were his life-line.

"Why the library? Most people would go around to the landmarks in town and snap selfies to show they'd been there." Dozens of tourists visited, many for the annual town festivals or for the peak weekend viewing of the autumn leaves. He'd never met a tourist who came to Cedar Grove for the express purpose of visiting the library.

"I was planning on going to the court-house, but a funny thing happened, and I changed my mind. When I returned to my room after dinner, a book was on the floor. I must have knocked it off the table acciden-tally."

"I don't understand. How would that change your destination?"

"It was Jane Austen's *Sense and Sensibility*. One of my favs. It had fallen open and I spotted the discarded book stamp from the local library. The book is dated 1813. An original." She spoke with awe and reverence, but it didn't explain her presence in the media room.

"What am I missing? I mean, an original is great, but Jason has lots of amazing treasures at the inn."

"It's actually quite simple. I realized if Cedar Grove had a library then, there was a good chance they might have had a newspaper. I asked Kyle this morning and he told me about the *Gazette*. I want to check the microfilm to find when the paper first went to print. I'm following up on a hunch." Her smile brightened the room.

Blake got up and crossed the room to stand next to her. "The first paper was printed in 1805, shortly after the town incorporated. It just so happens I'm researching the publications in the early 1800s. Maybe I can help find what you're looking for."

Her look of surprise at his offer reminded him of what a jerk he'd been yesterday. Things were just things, even if they were antiques. It was people who counted, and the very reason he was researching his family's genealogy.

"Oh, that's right. You're the history buff in town. I shouldn't have been surprised to see you here based on Jason's comments. I'm researching family history and I'm sure you have better things to research—like war. Isn't that what most men are interested in when it comes to history?"

It didn't help that the brunette set off his man radar, her long hair draped softly to one side of her beautiful face, cascading down past her shoulders. But it was her freckles and dark blue eyes that captured his attention the most. Blake was a sucker for freckles. Unfortunately, his appreciation hadn't carried over into their short conversation yesterday.

Nothing shouted "take notice" to him louder than a woman into history, especially one who would sacrifice her vacation and hide herself away in a library digging up the past. He shook his head to focus on her words and not her mouth. "That makes two of us—researching family, not war." Blake ignored the *most men* comment, his interest growing by the minute. "You have family from Cedar Grove? I've never seen you around the area before."

"Maybe. Maybe not. It's a long story." She shrugged.

Evasive or truthful, he wasn't sure which, but it didn't squash his curiosity, not by a long shot. "Try me. I'm due for a break and a good story."

"I doubt it, but here's the edited version. I was cleaning out my great-grandmother's attic and found an old trunk. Inside, I found a note tucked between the pages in a leather-bound book. It referenced the Crestfield Inn and was dated the night my great-grandmother's great-grandfather died. The signature was CW and I want to find who that person is and hopefully, why they wrote the note."

"That's a lot of *greats* ago. What's the signif-icance of the note?" She had his complete interest. After all, unraveling the past was what he loved most, and this was right up his alley.

"Don't say I didn't warn you. It's com-plex. Captain Tremont would be my great-grandfather six times removed to be exact. The story handed down through the generations is that Captain John Tremont was a decorated war hero from the War of 1812 and the Battle of Lake Champlain in 1814. They say he ventured out into a stormy night not fit for man nor ship and that his gunboat capsized. The Navy court martialed him for smuggling, citing it as the only reason a naval officer of his caliber would have been out that night, and he was dishonorably dismissed. And all this hap-pened after his death.

He was buried without honor, and with-out a pension for the infant daughter left behind. And the bounty typically bestowed upon an officer and hero for service to his country never happened. It is said distant relatives raised the girl, but the stories handed down through the generations tell of the heavy price she paid for her father's mistakes. The note gives me reason to believe there might've been another reason he ventured out that night, and I'm here to see if I can unravel the mystery. Now are you sorry you asked?" Sarah grinned.

She had become animated as she told the story, her eyes shining with a passion he rarely saw in others. Her eagerness to discover the past equaled his own, and right then and there, he knew, if she'd let him, he wanted to help her find the truth.

"His poor daughter. It's unfortunate, but these things happened far too often back then. What makes you think no one knew about the note or investigated when all this took place?"

"Because I have the note. If the military's investigation knew about it, it would have confiscated and claimed as a part of their records. But since they didn't, it leads me to believe they never knew about its existence. Not to mention, the story has never made sense to anyone who hears it. No one can figure out why a decorated war hero would start smuggling, and in all the stories I've heard told over the years, none ever mention this note."

"Sounds reasonable. When did he die?"

Sarah pulled an envelope from her purse and removed a document. "Here's the note. You can see for yourself and tell me what you think."

Blake took fragile piece of paper, using extra care knowing it was an irreplaceable dated piece of history.

May 24th, 1815
Leaving Crestfield Inn. Don't follow. Mind made up.
C.W.

"Interesting."

"Why interesting?" Her gaze locked with his, her brow drawn tight.

"Mainly the coincidence. You're researching the people of this town and events in 1815, and I'm researching the people and events in this town from the same time frame. I'm currently in 1845 and winding my way back to the late 1700s when people first settled the area."

"And what's your reason for dredging up the past? Other than your love for history?" He watched her fight back the grin threatening to escape, a fight she eventually lost.

"Don't laugh. Just because I look and act like a geek doesn't make me a geek."

"I never said that." A warm blush filled Sarah's cheeks.

She wasn't as immune to him as she might want to be—information he'd keep stored away for another time. Aside from their first meeting, he couldn't deny his interest.

"It's your turn to tell. What are you researching?" She was persistent, another admirable trait except when used against him.

"My family tree." Not the most exciting answer coming from a guy, but the truth. It was probably about as exciting as taking a woman to a museum on their first date. For the woman anyway. And if Perry were to be believed, any hope of taking Sarah on a date could now be rubber stamped with one word.

History.

"Okay. Maybe I should have reserved my geek judgement until I knew more about you." She bit her lip, but in the end, she failed miserably to keep from laughing.

"Thanks. Guess that means any hope of taking you to dinner tonight has been destroyed." He couldn't resist tossing out the feeler to see where he stood.

"I don't remember being asked so it's a moot point. Back to the note—what do you make of it?"

"It's rather vague. But you never know, and luck has a lot to do with deciphering history." She'd evaded his round-about invitation nicely, but she hadn't said no. And by the looks of things, he'd have plenty of time to ask again if they were both going to be at the library all day.

"That's what I thought. Why aren't you teaching today?"

"The kids are off —teacher workday. What do you say to us joining forces while you're in town and helping each other cover the material?"

"Even though I'm a destroyer of history, you want to work with me?" She rolled her eyes.

"I know you didn't mean it. And if I hadn't been having such a difficult day, things might've been done differently. I'm sorry I was such a bear. How about if we start over?" He held out his hand, hoping she'd accept his proposition.

"Okay, antique man, you've got yourself a deal."

She made him sound old with her not-so-endearing endearment. The term antique man was the new least-favorite thing he'd ever been called.

"You haven't happened to come across anyone with the initials CW, have you? It would make my life easy." Her grin was infectious, and Blake was glad he'd made the offer.

This could prove interesting before the day was over. "Not that I'm aware of, but I will pay more attention going forward—or backward, depending how you look at it. Why don't you start with the first paper in 1805?" He walked over to the filing cabinet and removed some folders from the back.

"Here. These files will cover 1805 to 1815." He handed her the stack.

"Where are you in your research?" Sarah glanced over to where he'd been working.

"Courthouse records only date back to the mid-1800's since it wasn't until then they started documenting births and deaths, at least in Vermont. I traced everything to a Matthew Lawrence and now I'm looking for a birth announcement, hoping to identify his parents." "Okay, that's easy enough to watch for."

"The society pages seemed to have the most useful information, so I've been sticking to them for the most part." It was true, but history had a way of sidetracking his well-intentioned efforts.

"Meaning?"

"There are some good stories that catch my eye and I can't resist reading them. Slows things down a bit but..." He shrugged.

"But to the history buff, it's like chocolate to a chocoholic." She had him pegged even though they'd just met.

"You got it. As to your search, you said the note mentioned the Crestfield Inn. Is it possible your person isn't from around here and was a guest at the inn?" Blake wasn't trying to dissuade her from her search, but it made sense to point out other possibilities.

"I've considered that, but two things stand to reason. One, Captain Tremont lived right across the lake. What are the odds it would have been some random stranger passing through town writing to him, as compared to knowing someone who lived here?" Sarah took a seat at the other reader and flipped on the lamp to illuminate the screen.

"Good point. What's number two?"

She let out a deep breath. "There isn't one, except I have nowhere else to search."

"Another good point." He liked her attitude. *Maybe Perry was right*. It was time to change things up a bit and taking Sarah out would be a fine place to start.

"I wanted to talk to Jason last night, but he had some emergency at the inn. I thought I'd catch up with him later today. I'm hoping he has some of the inn's old ledgers, if any have survived over the years. If I can look through them, maybe I can rule out CW as a guest. It could be the inn was a meeting place, or maybe the person worked at the inn. I honestly don't know what to think. I'm hoping by going through the Gazette, I'll at least have a better picture of life in Cedar Grove back then."

When he woke up this morning, he never would have expected the direction the morning had taken. Working together with Sarah sounded like fun. He'd always loved history, but this was history with a new twist.

Chapter Three

♥

SARAH STOOD UP TO stretch, frustrated with the futility of the hours she'd spent scrolling through the reader, with nothing to show for it except strained eyes from trying to decipher the articles and tight back muscles from hunching over the machine. "I was hoping things would go a little better than this. I can't believe neither one of us has found a single thing of interest."

"Look on the bright side—we've managed to knock out a few more years on either end, closing the gap of time. We only have forty years or so to cover between us." Blake laughed, the warm sound easing some of her tension. "Besides, anything worth having is worth putting in the effort. History is something we piece together. Be patient."

Mr. Upbeat and Cheery to the rescue, but he did have a point. It was easier for a history geek to find the fun in this, while she on the other hand, preferred dealing with action and suspense, the thrill of the next scene always around the bend. "I wouldn't say patience is one of my virtues. When I set my mind to something, I want it done. Time is not my friend."

For the next hour or so, Blake tried to make her laugh with stories from the past, making the time pass quicker. Not at all what she expected from him, but more than welcome. When she first planned out this trip there was no way she could have foreseen the direction her research would take, but the man next her made it fun. His easy-going manner allowed her to relax. After all, she was just a tourist. Here today, gone tomorrow. Or five days from now.

And the fact he'd teasingly asked her out and then dropped the subject hadn't gone unnoticed. Maybe that's why she'd let her guard down. They could be friends.

Sarah rubbed the back of her neck and looked over at Blake. "I see what you mean about not being able to resist reading the articles. This is incredible. And the outfits in the nineteenth century are as entertaining as the ads. I can't imagine what it was like to live in such tough times."

"I agree. Life was completely different than it is today, and with none of the conveniences we take for granted." Blake leaned back in his chair, watching her.

"True. It was an age of no computers or internet. An age when horses and buggies were the normal mode of transportation, and when entertainment was based on high society balls and gambling halls, instead of dinner and a movie or concert. But reading these stories makes me feel the history in a way I never understood."

"Bingo. That's one of the reasons I love doing this kind of research. I think you've earned a break. Why don't we go to Bixby's and grab some lunch? It'll help us regroup, save our eyes, and keep us from leaving with a monster headache by the time the day is over."

His suggestion sounded fabulous, anything to take a break from the history, her curiosity about the modern-day man sitting next to her far more interesting. "I could use a bit of food. Is it far? I walked, but these heels aren't suitable for any long-distance treks. Do you have a car, or maybe even a horse and buggy parked out front?"

"It's a car, smart aleck, but it's not out front. I use my bike in town. The car is for when I visit my mother over in Bellevue or run into Burlington. You should be all right. It's not far and we can cut through the parking lots to make it easier." Blake stood and flipped off his reader lamp.

Sarah did the same before grabbing her purse of the table. "Lead on."

"We're leaving for lunch, Perry. We'll be back to pick up where we left off and clean up."

"Okay. Thanks for letting me know. Didn't know you two knew each other?" He looked back and forth between them with interest.

"We don't. Not really. But I'm working on it." Blake grinned and turned to leave.

She looked between the two men, shook her head, and started to follow, wondering what Blake meant.

"Sounds like you're taking my advice," Perry called out after them.

Blake stopped, turning back to the librarian. "Which was?"

"Well, for starters, there's no food at the museum." Perry couldn't hide his grin, but it was Blake's chuckle that tipped her off it was an inside joke. Over lunch, she intended to find out what Perry meant.

Blake's hand pressed against the small of her back as she passed through the front door. A small gesture, but one she loved in a guy. Women's liberation was great, but not at the expense of the special little things a gentleman did for a lady out of care and concern. And something she hadn't had the pleasure of experiencing in quite a while.

They walked side by side down the steps. At the bottom, Blake steered her to the left. The early-afternoon sun warmed her face, a pleasant change after the stuffy media room.

They rounded the corner of the library, cutting across the lawn, and then walked across the parking lots that were accessed off Main Street. She suddenly remembered where she'd seen Bixby's, having walked past it last night on her way to the tavern for dinner.

A woman in the parking lot waved at them and headed their way. Dressed in a dark blue jacket and matching skirt, a white silk blouse, and dark blue heels, she was every bit the businesswoman. Even her hair had been pulled back in a tight bun, showing off a smooth complexion covered in heavy makeup. "Hey, Blake. Are you enjoying your day away from the kids at school?"

"Good afternoon, Alicia. You betcha. The microfilm reader and I have been on an intense date all morning at the library."

"Of course. Where else would you be? I'm surprised you haven't stopped in this week." Alicia's light and flirty laugh grated on Sarah's nerves. It was obvious the woman had the hots for Blake, the excessive sweetness in her voice a dead giveaway.

"Why? Are there any new listings I need to know about?"

"No. At least, not in the price range you set. Sorry. Maybe we should go over the numbers again?" Give the woman an E for effort, but an F in futility. Blake was clueless.

"No problem. I can be a patient man." He winked at Sarah. She knew he was poking fun at her earlier reference to being anything but patient, but she'd forgive him anything when he turned his smile on her.

"I'm just trying to help." Alicia's voice had become tight, the hint of a frown etched between her brows.

"Keep me posted. We're going to have lunch at the diner. Sarah is doing some historical research on her family, and we've decided to team up on a project together while she's in town."

On second thought, maybe he *wasn't* clueless. *Maybe...he wasn't interested.* The thought gave Sarah immense pleasure, although why, she had no idea. And it was better not to think about it.

"Oh. Are you staying long?" The woman's gaze drifted her way, as if noticing Sarah for the first time. Alicia's territorial claws were exposed, the subtle warning in her voice designed to establish her claim.

"As long as it takes." Sarah pursed her lips, fighting the grin threatening to escape. She was leaving Wednesday morning bright and early—information that was none of Alicia's business.

"I see." The uptight blonde saw what she wanted to see—not that it mattered. The history teacher was handsome in his own geeky way, but it didn't mean Sarah's interest extended beyond normal male appreciation.

"Later." Blake lifted his hand in farewell. He reached out and took Sarah's arm, leading her toward the diner. "Hope you don't mind my forwardness, but it was a great opportunity to send her a not interested message. She's been a little more aggressive lately in trying to force the idea of the two of us together."

Sarah didn't mind at all. In fact, she was flattered. Instead of pulling her arm away, she left it right where it was, content to be close by his side. "You're looking at buying property?" Small talk was always a safe avenue. Anything else, like questions about Alicia or why he hadn't dropped her arm yet, would be out of line—no matter how much she wanted to ask.

"I am. I live in the apartment complex not far from the inn. It's close to the school, but I've reached a point in my life where I feel like I need more than a bachelor pad. I'd like a place to call my own. Unfortunately, in a town this small, there's not a lot of property available. Most of these are historic homes and don't change hands often. Those that are on the market are priced steeper than I'm willing to go. It'll work itself out eventually." He shrugged but kept walking.

"Here we are." He let her arm go but only long enough to place it at the small of her back again as he led her through the door—leaving it there as he guided her toward a booth. "You're in for a treat. Katrina's creations are known county wide. And make sure you don't leave town without having some of her fresh donuts and pastries. She's usually sold out of those by ten every morning."

"The inn serves breakfast and it would be hard to give up Eggs Benedict for a donut—no matter how good the donut."

"True. Jason hired an amazing chef. He used to be one of New York's finest before he moved to town and Jason lucked out getting him. But Katrina, she's a local, and that woman can cook a mean meal. Trust me."

A pretty girl, in her late teens, approached the booth and smiled. She handed them the two menus.

"Hey, Mr. Carter." She eyed Sarah, a question lingering in their depths. She turned to Blake, the smile never slipping from her face. "Today's special is a Shrimp Mac and Cheese. Or would you like to order something else?"

"What do you say, Sarah? Think you can handle the special?" Blake's condescending smile irked her.

Shrimp, macaroni, and cheese sounded positively disgusting mixed together, but the idea of backing from his dare sounded worse. "Are you having it?" No sense going in all the way if he wasn't going to sacrifice his lunch.

"Absolutely. Like I said, there's not much Katrina makes that doesn't sit right with me." The gleam in Blake's eyes pushed her over the edge.

"I guess that settles it—two orders of the special please. And I'll have a water." Sarah wanted to order three waters to wash away the flavor, but she'd settle for refills.

"Water for me also. Thanks, Carrie." He handed the girl the menus and she shuffled off. "She's one of my students. I can tell she's quite curious about you, and I'm sure I'll be subjected to an inquisition on Monday."

Blake had lowered his voice and shot her an all-knowing look.

"Nothing you can't handle, I'm sure."

He leaned against the back of the cushioned seat bench. "Now that we've established that you're adventurous and daring—at least in your food choices, why don't you tell me something about you I don't know." His charming smile made her forget about the food and she turned her full focus on him. It was a pleasant change of pace from her ordinary pace and there was no harm in sharing. "For starters, I live just across the lake, in Plattsburgh. I can be home in under two hours if there aren't any tractors hogging the road and going ten miles per hour, and, of course, if the ferry has favorable crossing conditions."

"I know the area. We've taken some school field trips over to some of the battlefield memorials."

"Of course you have." Teasing him about his over-the-top thirst for history was fun.

"Let's see." She tapped a finger on her chin trying to decide how much to share. "I own a small cottage where I spend most of my time sitting on my front porch and writing, gazing out over the lake." The place might be small, but it was her own and it left her dependent on no one.

But more importantly, it afforded her the privacy she needed to focus on her stories, capturing the spirit of the plot and the characters, and bringing them to life.

"Lakefront? Nice. What do you mean by *writing*?"

Carrie delivered their waters and left, but Sarah noticed when the girl reached the register, she and another girl glanced in their direction. *Busted.* They looked away and pretended to straighten menus.

"I write romantic suspense and mysteries. In fact, I'm thinking about writing Captain Tremont's story if I can figure out what happened. I could turn it into a diabolical mystery, bordering somewhere between truth and fiction."

"That sounds great. I've never met a writer before. What started you down that path and have you published much? Would I have heard of you?" He leaned forward, as if genuinely interested in her answer.

Sarah shrugged. "Probably not. Unless, of course, you make a habit of reading romance. And I only have four published so far." It had been a long road to publication, but worth every minute of the learning curve. Well, except for learning her last boyfriend thought she would be a catalyst to his career venture into writing. Not to mention unfaithful.

Blake shook his head. "Can't say that I do— but I could start. Do you use a pen name or your own?"

"It's a pen name. Agatha Burns. But you don't have to look me up because I can promise there's nothing you'd like." She couldn't believe she'd told him the name.

Only her closest friends and family knew the truth, mostly because she wanted to keep that part of her life separate. But talking to Blake, she was comfortable. Way more comfortable than she felt selling herself and marketing her books—her least favorite part of the process. Sarah by far preferred to stay focused, or lost in, as the case may be, on the writing part.

"I'll be the judge. When you're not writing, what do you do?" When he gazed at her with his big, brown eyes and long lashes from behind the glasses that magnified every detail, she found herself ready to tell him anything he wanted to know.

Telling strangers about herself wasn't her normal mode of operation, but after the morning they shared—nothing about Blake was strange—unless you counted his deep love for old things.

"I'm part of a small group at church, and our focus is communing with God while in the great outdoors. We like to hike, bike wooded trails, kayak, and go birding. Sometimes my stories are the result of those trips. You'd be surprised the wild notions and scenarios a few of us can create out in the backwoods when crazy things happen."

"Like what?"

"I remember once when we were kayaking, we got caught in a pop-up lightning storm. We were in the middle of a forest, and the river was the only way from point to point. Our choices were tall trees or water, which in a lightning storm means no choice.

In between disagreeing on what to do, hard-headed people, and mother nature—it was not a fun race down the river for safety. But it was the perfect set up for a couple of bad guys to be chasing us in my second book."

"Nice. Sounds intense. Maybe that's the one I should read."

"I don't guarantee you'll like it, but I do guarantee a happily-ever-after."

"Nothing wrong with a happy ending."

The bell on the door tinkled repeatedly, the diner a non-stop place of customers coming and going. She'd noticed most people stopped and talked to others, always with a ready smile on their faces. Blake was a part of this town and judging by the people who stopped to say hi or wave, he was well-liked.

"What about you? What do you do when you're not researching genealogy or teaching history?" She sat back, more than casually interested in his answers.

"If I'm not researching history, I'm reading about history. It's just something I picked up as a kid and it stuck. Sometimes, I visit my mother or hang with friends, but Rushton High keeps us active socially year-round with school events or local festivities. They always need volunteers and a single man might as well be wearing a sign saying *I'm available*, or so I'm told. The committees like the muscle and the body count, and the participants, well, the ladies, they like the men." The flush of color in his cheeks endeared him to her more.

He wasn't one of those arrogant handsome men who thought the world owed him. *Unlike her ex.* "I see. You're one of those all-around good guys." No wonder Alicia felt the need to send a territorial warning, even if it was a one-sided attraction. If Sarah lived here, she might have been tempted to take a shot at him for herself. Before Larry came along that is and soured her on relationships completely.

He shook his head and shrugged. "I wouldn't say that, but I suspect it's what others think."

"Tell me one thing that would make you a devilish rogue." Everything about Blake shouted nice guy. She leaned in closer, waiting to hear some dirt on him.

"How's this?" He leaned forward and reached for her hand. "I only met you yesterday and I've thought of kissing you."

Well then. Perhaps she'd misjudged him, because nothing could have shocked her more. It was flattering. Although, she'd promised herself no more entanglements and needed to set the record straight with Blake. Relationships were complicated, and she didn't have time for complicated.

The server approached the table with their meals, saving Sarah from having to respond. She pulled her hand back to make room in front of her for the plate. Keeping her eyes glued on the strange concoction otherwise known as lunch made it easy to avoid Blake's gaze. She picked up her fork and stirred the casserole, trying to gather the courage to take the first bite.

Blake dug in without any hesitation. *"Hmmm.* You won't regret trying it, I promise."

Finding it easier to face him than take a bite, she looked up. "And if I do? Regret it, that is." She was stalling the inevitable.

"I'll make a bet with you. If you like it, you agree to have dinner with me tonight when we finish our research. If you don't like it, you have the choice of whether to have dinner with me or not." The twinkle in his eyes matched his grin. Blake was up to no good and testing the success of his earlier comment about going to dinner.

Overriding the voice of reason, Sarah shook her head and laughed. "Another roundabout dinner invitation? Sounds to me like you win either way." It was flirting, but what the heck. He wasn't asking for a lifetime commitment, just dinner. And she hadn't agreed to go.

"I was hoping—but thanks for confirming what I already suspected." Any resistance she might have had disappeared.

"And what is it you suspect?" Nothing could have stopped her from asking the question.

"You like me too. Maybe enough you've also thought of kissing me." She hadn't, but that didn't mean his comment wouldn't be the catalyst to make it happen.

"Don't push your luck, mister. Maybe I would agree simply because I don't want to eat dinner alone.

He grinned, taking another bite of his lunch, and making a big show of sliding the fork in his mouth, savoring the food as if it were heavenly.

The only smart thing left to do was stuff her mouth with food to keep her from talking because then she might actually admit to the fact, she was thinking about it now. She raised the fork, slowly, dragging out the inevitable. Her nose and mouth scrunched in disgust as she slid the fork in her mouth.

Instead of the nasty, I-need-to-spit-this-out moment she expected, she found herself enjoying the delicious creamy cheese sauce and the shrimp flavors all rolled together. She took another bite. And another.

"*Hmmm.*" No one would ever believe her when she told them, but this was by far her new favorite way to have macaroni and cheese, the dish baked to perfection. "This is amazing. I may have to come to Cedar Grove just to have this again. I doubt there's anywhere in Plattsburgh that serves anything remotely close to this."

Blake chuckled. Leave it to him to be one of those gloaters, rubbing in the fact he'd won and had been right. "I'm glad you like it. And I guess my dinner date for tonight is now confirmed."

Sarah was ready to agree to his invitation but some part of her held back. The not-so-trusting part. "Tell me something first. What did Perry mean when he said you were taking his advice? It sounded like some guy code comment between the two of you."

His grin widened. "It's not as bad as you think. He was giving me a tough time about taking women on a date to a museum. Thinks I should change things up a bit."

"What's wrong with a date to a museum?" She frowned, not understanding the problem.

"Exactly my point. Nothing. Or should be nothing. It's a wonderful place to walk and talk and learn about someone without pressure." Blake shrugged and then took another bite of the creamy mac and cheese.

"Learn about someone? As in a first date?"

"Yes. Why?"

"No wonder you're single. Not the most romantic place you can take a woman for a first date. Perry is right. Sorry."

Blake's sudden grin caught her off guard. "Then it's a good thing we're going to dinner for our first date."

She hadn't come to Cedar Grove looking to spend time with a guy but judging by his comment it might work out that way. And for the life of her, she couldn't figure out how it would be a bad thing. Maybe a temporary hiatus was in order for her rules.

Research and fun for the next four days. Who could say no? Perhaps both elements would help her write the next story with spot-on accuracy. History and a few stolen kisses. For research purposes, of course.

"I know you said you didn't have a chance to talk to Jason last night, but do you want to run by there before we head to the library? He's a good friend of mine, and I'm sure between the two of us we can convince him to give you access to whatever you need."

"That would be awesome. Thank you."

The server dropped off the bill and Sarah reached for it. Blake's hand landed on top of hers, the warmth of his skin sizzling against hers.

"Not on my watch. My treat since I invited you." The steely determination in his voice was reason enough for Sarah to back down. His mother had taught him well, and right now, she was the direct beneficiary of all those lessons.

Chivalry wasn't dead, and she liked it.

They walked side-by-side toward the Crestfield Inn. Jason and Kyle stood behind the counter; their heads bent together as they poured over a ledger.

"Jason, just the guy we need to see." Blake leaned against the counter as Jason came around the desk to join them.

"Sorry I couldn't break away to talk to you last night, Sarah. What's up with you two? I hadn't realized you knew each other judging by yesterday's encounter on the front porch." He looked back and forth between them.

"Don't worry about it. I'm spending the day at the library, chipping away at time." She laughed at her own joke. "And no, we didn't know each other before yesterday, but I ran into Blake at the library. Apparently, you weren't far off the mark when you talked about him being buried in history.

He was deep into 1845 when I ran into him." She winked at Jason, but Blake noticed it, a look of irritation flashing across his face.

"Don't let her fool you, she's here for the history too. She's spent the morning buried in 1805 to 1810." Blake bumped shoulders with her, giving her a slight push.

"What on earth are you two talking about?" Jason shook his head, trying to make some sense of their nonsense.

"It seems we're both currently in the process of researching Cedar Grove history. Hers involves the Crestfield Inn, and mine as you know, is a genealogical thing. We've decided to help each other with the research to expedite the process."

"I see, I think. How does your research involve the inn and what do you need from me?" Jason didn't seem surprised at all by the turn of events, or at least he didn't show it.

Sarah filled him in on the story about Captain Tremont and about the note. "I was hoping you might've come across old ledgers that I can go through to see if I can find any guests who might match those initials. At this point I don't know if it was a guest, someone working here, or someone living in the area. I'm winging it."

"There's a ton of old information in the attic, stored away. I've not had enough time to go through it all since I've been focused on the remodel and reopening of the inn. Kyle has a key and will give it to you whenever you want to go have a look."

"Thanks. We haven't come across anything this morning but hopefully it'll be a more productive afternoon, and speaking of that, we need to head back to the library." Blake moved close to her, his hand landing on her back again as he guided her toward the door.

"Maybe after we finish at the library I'll go and poke around the attic, depending what we find." Wednesday would arrive far too fast and she didn't want to waste time in searching for answers.

"You have a dinner date as I recall," Blake said, daring her to refute his claim.

"But there's no guarantee how long it will last," she teased.

"You two sure have come a long way since yesterday." Jason's grin spoke volumes. "Wouldn't have believed it if I didn't see it with my own two eyes."

"At the time, I had no idea she was into history. A most attractive quality in a woman if you ask me." Blake's light-hearted laughter echoed through the lobby as he took her by the arm and escorted Sarah toward the door.

Chapter Four

♥

THE NORMAL LIBRARY QUIET rules were ignored as they researched and talked—some history related, and some more personal in nature. When Sarah had started on this project, nothing could have prepared her for the reality of Blake and the fun she would digging into the 1800s, although a good part of what made it easy was more than likely directly related to the man himself.

Having spent more time with her writing and books and less time with people, his flirtatious comments left her reeling and against her better judgement, hopeful he'd continue. It was flattering to have such an attractive man show interest, and the fact he could make her laugh, priceless.

Blake wasn't anything like Larry, which made it harder to remember why she'd made the rules in the first place. And it became harder to focus on the microfilm, but being in Cedar Grove was temporary, something that would be dangerous to forget. The real world of deadlines awaited her back home.

There was no place for her in Cedar Grove, and no matter how tempting, starting a long-distance relationship would be a fool's folly. It would require tremendous amounts of trust and a heavy time commitment, something Sarah wasn't prepared to give anyone.

"Hey, Blake. I found another W last name to add to our list. Westerly. Owen Westerly. I think we're up to five, or is that six?"

"That's five. Weston. Wayne. Wright. Web. And now, Westerly. Got it." He jotted the name down in his notebook. "What's his story?"

"He died in 1813. Looks like he owned the Cedar Grove logging company and sawmill. It doesn't list a cause of death."

"Back then I doubt they cared much about the reason unless it was obvious or noteworthy, like a gunshot wound or the plague."

"Not unlike our media today—sensationalism at its finest." She nodded her head as she exchanged an all-knowing look with Blake. "Oh, but it does say he was survived by two daughters. No names are listed, but they would be two more possibilities to check into." She rolled her shoulders and stretched her neck, the muscles stiff from sitting.

"There are two cemeteries in town that existed in the early 1800s, St. Mary's and the First United Presbyterian. They're big and it could take quite a bit of time, especially since some of the headstones might be broken, or the engraving worn and not legible.

How long are you planning on staying?" He looked up from his machine, fixing her with a smile.

"Till Wednesday. There must be an easier way to narrow this down."

"I thought it sounded like you were planning to be here a while. I must have misunderstood." *Nope.* He understood what she'd said to Alicia perfectly, but he didn't know why she'd said it.

Thank goodness. Blake was a kind, down-to-earth, and funny guy. The hardest kind of man to resist when they turned on the charm. "I've got a few deadlines for some promotional stuff that I need to work on."

"*Hmmm.* It might be faster if we check any existing church records first. I'm sure you'd prefer to sit behind a desk and scrounge through ledgers than traipse through the cemeteries."

More than he knew. "Good idea. I did that once in a mystery novel—used the church records to find out more about the killer's family to figure where he might run and hide."

"Thankfully, we're not dealing with a killer. I'm starting to wonder about you and what you write."

Sarah choked on her water. It wasn't the first time she'd heard those words and it probably wouldn't be the last, but they never cease to catch her off guard when they came. "What's a good suspense or mystery without a murder?"

"If you say so. I can pick up the newspaper and read about thugs, death, and destruction every day. Not my idea of entertainment."

"Ah, but you see there's one big difference—mine all end happily-ever-after."

"Not for the guy who died. Any chance one of your books would be here? Perhaps a change of pace from history to love and murder would be good for my late-night reading material." He might be teasing, but then again, with Blake, one couldn't be sure.

"Doubtful. You'd have to look online. Do you want to go in the morning?"

"That'll work. Sunday they'll be busy and might not want to deal with us poking our nose into their history."

"Perfect. We have a date at the church."

He shook his head and laughed. Chalk another one up for Blake—he got her sense of humor.

"With a possible stop at the cemetery. Hopefully, your next book doesn't include a quick marriage and the groom mysteriously dying soon after."

She stopped to look over at him and shake her head. "Would I do that?" She fought back a grin, hoping to maintain a look of innocence.

"I'm beginning to think so."

"You'll have to read my next book to find out, won't you?"

"Guess I will." He chuckled and turned to his reader to focus on the article splashed across his screen.

Sarah followed suit, her grin wide enough to leave an aching in her cheeks.

Focused on the articles, she discovered several weekly issues missing during the period of the War of 1812 and the Battle of Lake Champlain. Those that were published held fewer stories in the society pages, the paper mostly dedicated to the war. She remembered reading about the battles in her high school history class, but this came across as personal. More intense. More real.

She turned to the society page and scanned the entries. Her gaze caught and held on one word—Westerly.

"Jackpot!" A chill of excitement raced down her spine.

"What does it say?" Blake stopped his search and looked over at her.

"There was a house fire on May 10, 1815. It mentions the Westerly's will be residing at the Crestfield Inn while their home is being reconstructed. What if these are the daughters of Owen Westerly and they were staying at the inn? I never considered the possibility they could be locals and staying there."

Blake stood and stretched before coming to stand next to her. "This is great."

"It doesn't give names, but I have a good feeling about this. I hate that we need to wait until morning to check the church records. It will drive me insane with curiosity." She stood, barely checking her jubilation, and throwing herself into Blake's arms.

"I agree it sounds good, but it doesn't mean a thing. Not yet, anyway. There are four other W's on this list, and there's no telling which one it might be, if any."

"I know. But it's the first piece of information we've come across that gives us a second layer to the names and that plays out to a possible story that works."

"We've got about thirty minutes left before Perry closes shop. Let's keep going to make the best of our time."

"Yes, sir, Drill Sergeant Carter." She winked and sat down. "I know you're right."

"I like the sound of that."

"Which part?"

"All of it. Sir. Sergeant. Right. Works for me."

Sarah waded a piece of scrap paper and tossed it at Blake. A direct hit to the head and her smile, the only response needed.

Jump started by her find, she scanned page after page, hoping to find more information. Ten minutes later, she felt the familiar rush of excitement, this one more rewarding than the last. "Jackpot!" She couldn't believe her luck had struck twice in one day, but the headlines blazed at her.

Blake came to stand next to her. "You are one lucky lady today. Let's hear it."

"You won't believe it, but I found Captain Tremont mentioned in the *Gazette*. The headline reads, *Decorated War Hero Stops in Cedar Grove*. The article says he was on his way to Plattsburgh."

He leaned over her shoulder to peer at the screen, his hands on her shoulder for support. "That's fantastic. You have proof he's been in Cedar Grove. What does it say? I can't read it from this angle unless I sit in your lap." His laugh tickled against her ear.

"It goes on to tell about his efforts in the Battle of Lake Champlain and how they were honored he'd stopped in Cedar Grove for the night, staying at the Crestfield Inn and attending a ball that evening."

"The Crestfield? Now, that's solid information. What's the date of the article?"

"May 24th, 1815. Two weeks after the Westerly's began staying at the inn. Knowing the dates could help us zero in on what to look for in Jason's ledgers, assuming they exist and haven't been lost over the years.

Would you mind terribly if we checked there tonight?"

"Why, Sarah, my dear, are you requesting I accompany you on a date?" Blake bowed slightly, raising the back of her hand to press against his lips.

"Indeed, Sir Carter, I do believe I am." Falling in sync with his playacting had been easy, and she couldn't deny the flush of pleasure as she adopted a debutante role. They were two peas, but as bad luck would have it, in two different pods—in fact, the pods weren't even in the same field.

"Although I hold you in high regard, I'm afraid I must decline your sweet invitation as I'm already promised to another for the evening." The two of them burst out laughing.

"Perhaps, my good sir, you could reschedule your engagement and instead, spend the night with me." Her face flooded with warmth, the words coming out all wrong. "To do research, I mean," she corrected.

"I would be honored to accompany you, for I could never say no to a night with such a radiant beauty." The light in his eyes as he made his bold proclamation gave proof he was a fine actor, the role one that suited him.

"Hey, you two, break it up. This is a library. A library that's closing, I might add. Perhaps this non-date should be moved to a more appropriate date place." Perry stood guard at the door, grinning, keys in hand, and waiting for them to leave so he could lock up.

Guess she'd never know, the moment over.

Blake flipped off the lamps and gathered their belongings. "We're leaving. What's your rush? You got a hot evening planned?"

"You know I like to open and close on time."

"Yeah, yeah. Goodnight, and thanks for the advice." Blake grinned, clapping his friend on the shoulder as they passed him.

"Don't forget tomorrow is Saturday and I'm open from eight till noon. Did you have any luck today? With all that laughing and carrying on, I wouldn't expect you got much done."

"I had zero luck, but Sarah needs to buy a lottery ticket." Blake waved as they headed down the stairs.

Chapter Five

♥

BLAKE LED THE WAY to their first stop. Pizza. They'd agreed to grab something for dinner and camp out in the attic in search of the ledgers. She wanted to see what a date night with Blake would be like, but the attic would have to do for now. Finding information on Captain Tremont and gathering information for her story was the reason for her visit in the first place, and she needed to stay on track.

A big sign hanging from the front of the building announced they were at Murphy's. Judging by the lack of empty tables the place was a local favorite.

"Let's sit over here." He pointed to the long wooden counter where bar patrons sat watching sports on the big screen. "We can order and do take-out to speed things up."

"Sounds good. Do you come here often?" She had to raise her voice to be heard over the din of the crowd.

"Not many places to choose from in Cedar Grove, so yeah. How about a drink while we wait for our pizza? Consider it a celebration of your successful discoveries."

"I can do that. A glass of red wine please, preferably a blend or a cab." She sat on one of the stools and got comfortable, hanging her sweater across the back.

Blake discussed the dinner options with her, and they settled on the Murphy's special. She liked that he was considerate enough to ask, not that there was much she didn't like on pizza—except anchovies.

He placed the order for their food and drinks, and it wasn't long before the bartender slid their drinks in front of them.

Blake raised his glass of beer to offer her a toast. "To Owen Westerly and his daughters—may they be the ones."

"I'll drink to that." When the bill came, Sarah reached for it at the same time as Blake.

"I've got this." He tried to snag it out of her hand.

"Not this time, mister. My date, my treat." "Doesn't seem right, a woman buying a man's meal." Blake's grumbling didn't change her decision. It would appear antique man might be more aptly labeled Mr. Antiquated Man.

"This is the twenty-first century last time I checked. Women have come into their own, and since I did the asking—not to mention we're working on my stuff tonight, it's the least I can do. My date, my treat, and your rules." She grinned.

Blake shook his head and smiled, letting go of the bill. "Fine. But in the spirit of the twenty-first century, I should remind you, the next one is on me."

"Deal." They finished their drinks and it wasn't long before the pizza arrived, and they left, freeing up valuable real estate in the form of their seats.

They walked to the inn, Blake holding the door open when they arrived. The familiar scent of roses greeted her, warm and welcoming. Unfortunately, Kyle was nowhere to be found.

"We missed him and the attic's locked." They should have come straight here first.

"Follow me." Blake led her to another door and knocked, ignoring the private sign.

Jason answered the door. "What's up? Don't tell me you two are still working? You've been at this all day."

"She asked me on a date, and it would've been rude to say no."

Sarah wasn't going to let him fill Jason with nonsense. "Not exactly. I asked him to help me search for the ledgers and offered him food as an incentive and a reward. It always works with a man. We hoped you'd let us have the key to the attic. We found some dates and names today and I wanted to follow up on them. I think we're on to something."

"I figured it had to be something like that—our geeky history professor isn't exactly a lady-killer." Jason walked to the front reception desk, opened the drawer, and pulled out the key—handing it to Blake. "Who are you calling geeky? There's nothing wrong with being a history buff."

"Who said anything about history? I was referring to your penchant for polo shirts with sweaters over them, your wild hair, and your oversized 1970s' glasses." Jason shot Sarah a wink before heading down the hall, stopping at his door.

"I disagree. Sarah likes what she sees, don't you?" His teasing grin did nothing to ease the discomfort of being put on the spot.

"It doesn't matter what I like or don't like, leave me out of this." She did like what she saw but getting caught in the middle of whatever this was between friends or announcing the truth to Blake wasn't what she had in mind.

"See. I'm right. And don't forget you need to use the back stairs. Those are the only ones that go all the way to the attic. Check the boxes closest to the stairs marked Crestfield Inn. I've seen lots of books and ledgers, just haven't had the time to sort them. Try to be out by nine. I do have guests on the third floor and wouldn't want them disturbed after hours."

"A no answer doesn't make you right," Blake grumbled. Jason's smug smile made her want to correct his incorrect assumption, but she held back and instead followed Blake. It was a long climb up, Sarah stopping at the top and taking in a deep breath.

"Sitting behind a desk typing away all day doesn't keep me in stair-climbing shape."

"Quite the opposite for me—I'm always running after kids somewhere. Wait here. I'll unlock and switch the lights on."

Sarah shivered, a cold chill enveloping her. Odd, but just as quickly it was gone. She hoped she wasn't coming down with something. It was the same feeling she had yesterday when she first arrived. She didn't feel sick, but sometimes these things hit you unexpectedly.

"Room is open but it's warm in there. I can open the skylights if you get too hot. Jason's planning on finishing this room to use with the inn and installed them recently."

Sarah followed him into the attic. She looked around, her gaze taking in a veritable feast of antiques. There was everything from dressers and beds to spinning wheels and lamps, and everything in between. *Incredible.*

"This is an antique-dealers' dream."

"I agree. Jason's going through it little by little and incorporating what he can into decorating the inn. There's so much history stored here, it's amazing." The awe in his voice was unmistakable.

"I'm surprised you haven't taken over and moved in."

"I've thought about it a few times. There are even a few beds I could choose from, but I'll settle for sleeping in my own bed and helping Jason." He laughed.

"Creature comforts supersede history with you. Good to know."

"Can't deny it." Blake took two chairs off one of the tables in the corner and sat them next to each other.

Sarah placed a couple napkins under the pizza box and under their drinks, not wanting their dinner to leave any damaging marks on old, unwaxed wood.

They ate, Blake filling her in on life in modern-day high school. Things had certainly changed, and not necessarily for the better. He didn't like the current system, the tension in his voice, shoulders, and face, a triple giveaway. Less learning, less respect, and more entitlements, did not make for good preparation for a student to enter the adult world successfully.

One slice of pizza turned into two, as she listened to his view of the problems in the school system. What she discovered was a man who cared, not only about his students, but about the school and the town. And mostly, about the future of all three.

"You shouldn't have got me started on this subject. I'm sorry. I suppose we need to keep working. Don't forget, we only have until nine."

"It's okay. I've enjoyed hearing your take on everything. I'll start with the boxes on this side and you start with those. He said they should be near the door, but he forgot to mention there were forty or fifty boxes matching the description."

An hour later and they hadn't found a single journal. Her back hurt and she stood to stretch. Closing the lid of the box she'd been working on, she shoved it against the wall. "Maybe we should call it a night."

"I don't think so. It looks like it's my turn to call jackpot—even if technically it's for you. This box is full of journals." He started pulling out book after book and setting them on the dresser nearby.

Sarah crossed the room to help.

"I've got it! Here's the one for 1814 and 1815." Blake held it up for her inspection. Together they moved to sit down at the table, eager to inspect the ledger.

Blake flipped the pages one by one, his respect for history clear in the gentle touch he used.

"The writing is faded and hard to read in places." He slid the book in her direction. "Can you make any sense of it?"

She peered at the writing. August 1814. She flipped a few pages. December 1814. Sarah turned a few more pages knowing she had to be close. "I found it. Look. May 10th, 1815." She tapped the page at the entry. "C

Westerly checked into the Crestfield Inn. Two guests. This is it, I told you."

"I agree. This is compelling evidence pointing to the writer of your note, but unfortunately, it doesn't tell us who, or even if it's a man or a woman."

"But don't forget, Owen Westerly was survived by two daughters. We've not seen any male Westerly mentioned anywhere. At this point I would assume they're one in the same."

"True. We were already headed for the churches in the morning, and I think it's our best bet to discover C Westerly's birthday. Baptism records should be available. The churches were big on documenting information and if she was baptized, there should be a record of her name."

"This has been an amazing day. I feel bad because we're not making progress on your family history. Maybe to be fair, we should go to the library in the morning since they're only open a few hours. We can head to the churches afterward."

"I won't turn down the help if you're willing, but only if you're sure. I know how excited you are with this find, and I promise to help you check the church records either way."

Fair was fair, even if he was right about her excitement. She did prefer to skip the library, but she wouldn't tell him. Especially since spending time with Blake was fast becoming addictive. The sooner she found her information, the sooner she would leave town, and the sooner she'd go back to spending most of her time writing. And alone.

Helping Blake delayed the inevitable. "It's late. I'll take this ledger to my room and look through it for any other information that might help us, and we can meet in the morning." She clutched the book to her chest.

"Okay. Let me shut the lights off and lock this room."

He grabbed their dinner remnants and followed her out of the attic and down one flight of stairs to the second-floor hall, stopping in front of her door.

"Is this you?" Blake took a step closer.

"Yes. I can't begin to thank you enough for all your help."

"I've had fun." Before she had a chance to register what he was about to do, Blake leaned forward and dropped a kiss on her cheek. She mistakenly thought he was going to kiss her, as in on the mouth.

"Good night and sweet dreams. I'll meet you for breakfast downstairs at seven." He knew he'd thrown her for a loop, his devilish smile confirming it.

Turns out, Blake Carter was a rogue. The sweet and gallant kind of rogue romance novels loved something that made him perfect for her next story. Not that he'd want to know it.

"*Ummm*, I think that's for guests at the inn," she said, her brain still off-kilter from his friendly peck on the cheek.

"No worries. Jason's a friend, but if that doesn't work, just tell him I spent the night with you—working in the attic," he amended. He was back to teasing, his boyish grin cute.

"Good night." Long after he left, the sensation of his kiss remained, Sarah touching her cheek and wondering if he might like-like her. And if he did, did she feel the same?

Chloe liked the young man with Sarah. She'd noticed him before at the inn, but until now, she always dismissed the connection she'd felt when he came around. The man was quick on his feet and very much a flirt, much like she remembered the captain.

Sarah's eyes had lit with excitement, even if she wasn't ready to admit the level of attraction to her young man. Oh, to be young and free to pursue love. The only thing Chloe knew was unrequited love, the bane of her eternal existence. However, watching fresh sparks ignite between these two filled her with a warmth she hadn't experienced in forever.

Sarah needed a few nudges to push her in the right direction for her research—but maybe a few extra nudges to point her in the right direction with Blake would be in order.

Long after Sarah had turned out the lights and fell asleep, Chloe paid her another visit. Smart girl to doubt how the library book ended on the floor knowing full well she hadn't knocked it down, but luckily it hadn't stopped her from acting on the hint. Chloe wouldn't give up leading Sarah to the truth until the events of what really happened that night were revealed.

She crossed the room to the dresser where the ledger lay closed. Chloe flipped it open, letting the pages fall to May 24th, 1815. The same night

Captain Tremont stayed at Crestfield Inn and Chloe first laid eyes on the dashing gentleman. The same night she'd fallen in love. But it was never meant to be and doomed to remain a one-sided love affair, his heart taken by another that very night. Chloe was destined to remain in the shadows, the same as it had always been whenever her sister was around.

Chapter Six

♥

BLAKE ROSE EARLIER THAN usual, intent on jogging before he met Sarah. For only having known her two days, the connection he felt left him baffled. He'd never believed in love at first sight—still didn't. But love at second sight? He couldn't deny the remote possibility his friendship with her could lead to more. Either that or he'd been far too long without a meaningful relationship.

He hadn't been joking when he said a woman into history was an attractive quality. Add to that a woman who was beautiful on the inside and outside—that kind of woman was triple trouble to his heart.

He'd been in a handful of relationships and none of them had come close to making him feel about someone the way he felt about Sarah. Two days seemed ridiculous, but no matter how hard he tried to convince himself otherwise, he knew enough to realize he didn't want her walking out of his life Wednesday.

He'd tried long-distance once before, and it had failed miserably, but two hours wasn't a relationship killer. And when the woman was Sarah, he couldn't think of a single reason not to try.

After resisting the urge to kiss her for most of yesterday, giving in to a goodnight kiss had come to him as naturally as breathing. His first intention had been to kiss her on the mouth, but the last thing he wanted to do was send her running for cover by being too forward.

Her reaction gave him hope that come Wednesday, it might not be the last Blake saw of Sarah.

He strolled into the Garden Delight Café and spotted her at a table in the corner. With her hair drawn back and tied in a bun, her long slender neck and alabaster skin were a vision of loveliness. Her yellow blouse complemented the masses of adorable freckles dotting her face, freckles that one day he'd like to count and kiss.

"Good morning, gorgeous." He dropped a light kiss on her cheek, still not wanting to overstep his bounds.

"And a good morning to you. I'm glad you're here." Her eyes were shining with excitement and he couldn't wait to hear why.

"What's going on?" Blake sat in the chair next to her and poured a cup of coffee, refilling hers at the same time.

"I know you're going to think I'm crazy, but I talked to Jason this morning and he says I'm not. Crazy, that is." Her enthusiasm was contagious but beyond that, he was completely confused.

"Asked Jason about what?"

"Ghosts." She dropped her voice a notch as she uttered the word, as if she didn't want anyone else to hear.

Blake dealt in history, not ghosts. He'd never been much of a believer, although he'd heard the stories passed around town about a couple of local hauntings. Even Jason seemed convinced of their existence at the inn. It would be better to keep his skepticism to himself at this point. "What made you ask Jason and what was his answer?"

"I asked because I think I'm being visited by one of them." She sat back, her eyes locked on his face, watching for his reaction.

Not believing didn't mean he would diminish anyone else's belief to the contrary, especially not Sarah's. "Go on."

"He said there are several stories of ghosts at the inn and that he's heard some strange things since he moved in. No sightings, but odd things happen. Bettina Crestfield used to tell him stories about the ghosts, and she was a rock solid, no-nonsense kind of woman."

"You think you've seen the ghost?" Sarah had no reason to make the story up, no matter how farfetched it sounded. He needed to listen with an open mind.

"No, no. Nothing like that. But remember I told you about the library book on the floor? I don't think I knocked it there. I didn't say anything, but I'm more convinced than ever that I'm right." She added creamer to her coffee and stirred, and kept stirring, her gaze never leaving him.

"There might be other explanations. The housekeeper for one. Or a door slammed and knocked the book off the edge of the table." The realist in him had to try and rationalize the situation, not get carried away with it. It was one thing to listen with an open mind, another to commit to the same insanity. As a writer, Sarah's imagination would be like Merlin the Magician's—able to conjure up anything.

"True. But none of that would explain last night."

"I wondered when you were going to tell me what happened."

"After you left, I couldn't stay up and read. I put the book on the dresser, hoping to look at it this morning. When I woke, it was wide open."

"Maybe you were marking your place and forgot to close it? Or you're a sleepwalker. I don't know." He was trying hard to keep her grounded, but she wasn't budging from her position on the subject.

"Okay, funny guy. No, I'm not a sleepwalker. But since you don't want to be a believer, maybe you'll believe me when you hear the rest. Want to take a guess at the entry on the top of the page?"

"I have no idea, but I'm sure you're going to tell me." Blake's eyebrows shot up a notch, but he was listening, his curiosity fully engaged.

"It was the night Captain Tremont visited the inn. The records show he stayed four nights and that C Westerly was in residence."

"You're kidding." The coincidences were adding up—against his anti-ghost sentiments. History dealt with facts, but how did you deal with a ghost who also dealt with facts? Was it possible? There had to be some logical explanation, but at this point, he was fresh out of ideas.

"Would I kid about a thing like this? The article in the *Gazette* said the captain was passing through and we have proof he stayed longer than just passing through. Which means something, or someone, made him stay. And remember how the article mentioned a ball? What if he stayed and met someone? Someone like C Westerly and he fell in love. Maybe that's why she sent him a note. Maybe she had second thoughts and wanted to let him down gently."

"Okay, now you've gone off the deep end. I bet you're a fantastic romantic suspense writer." He refilled his cup of coffee after draining the first one. Caffeine was his best hope to keep up with Sarah's fanciful tale of love and intrigue, her imagination in high speed.

"As a matter of fact, I am, or so I've been told—but that's not why I'm jumping to this conclusion. All the pieces are adding up, and that's why I believe I'm we're close to the truth."

"Okay, what if I agree it's true and there's a ghost haunting the inn. Why you and why now?"

"I have no idea. It's not like I'm a ghost hunter or buster or whatever they are called. My experience amounts to zero."

"As does mine."

"Nice to see you both this morning. Here for a free meal, Blake?" Jason placed the breakfast plates on the table, pushing back some of the water glasses to make room.

"That and Chef Bryant's cooking. Sarah needs my help today. I'm making her pay for breakfast." They both laughed, knowing it was a lie since breakfast was complimentary for inn guests.

"More like he invited himself and said you wouldn't mind." She huffed. Her feigned irritation made them laugh harder.

"Enjoy. I'll leave you to your breakfast. I've got other guests to tend to who aren't as complicated as you two. Too early for this." He laughed and walked away.

Nothing was settled over breakfast, but the conversation hadn't been dull, not for a single moment. Shortly before eight, they left and headed for the library.

"Good morning, Perry."

"Good morning to you both. Back for more of the same?"

"Yes, but only because I promised to help Blake. He's not getting anywhere on his end of the research, and mine, well, let's just say, it's alive and kicking. I felt sorry for him."

Alive and kicking? She was making fun of him on several levels with her comment. *His history. Her ghosts. One dead and gone. One just dead.* But both coming to life the deeper they dug into the lives of the Westerly's and Captain Tremont.

"Is that a fact?" Blake didn't miss the wink his friend shot her way.

A twinge of jealousy rippled down his spine. No way. Blake made it a point to never do jealousy and he wasn't starting with Perry. "Depends who's telling the story." He wasn't letting her off the hook that easy.

"Go on you two. I've got work to do." Perry shook his head.

They headed for the media room and dropped their things on the table. Blake flipped on the reader lamps while Sarah pulled the files from the drawers.

"I guess we should pick up where we both left off."

"Sounds good. I'll turn you into a history geek yet." Blake sat down and loaded the microfilm into the machine.

"Don't count on it."

They laughed and joked for most of the morning, Blake ruling out year after year with no evidence of a birth announcement or any other mention of Matthew Lawrence.

He turned the wheel to the next week's paper society page. He scanned the page, the words Matthew Lawrence popping out to capture his attention. "You won't believe it, but I found Matthew."

"That's wonderful. What does it say?" Her voice rang with sincerity, proof this really was a team effort.

"Matthew Lawrence was born August 10th, 1842 to Caleb Lawrence and Teresa Johnson. That's a couple more links I can log on the tree. It's about time."

"And the best part is you can fast forward through the thirties and pickup right around 1825 to look for Caleb's parents. You've cut our workload by two-thirds."

"On that note, I'd say we've done enough for today. What do you say we head for the church offices?"

"If you're sure? Otherwise, we can stay longer."

"My history isn't going anywhere, and neither am I. The library will be here next Saturday. It's you that has to leave Wednesday, and I won't be much help come Monday morning because of school."

But until then, he intended to make the most of his time with Sarah.

♥

Chapter Seven

"WHICH CHURCH SHOULD WE go to first? You know this town better than I do." Sarah didn't have a preference and if it were up to her, she'd flip a coin.

"See, I told you I'd come in handy for something. I do happen to know the Catholic Church was more prominent when this area first settled, so if I was a guessing man trying to hedge my bets, I'd pick St. Mary's."

"That's a pretty in-depth picking process. Is there some brochure on the town where you read that little snippet?" She hadn't finished reading over all the material Kyle had given her upon arrival, but she was sure

Blake's history fetish was bound to come loaded with cool information.

She hoped he was right because combing the cemetery grounds wasn't high on her priority list. If they could isolate one, maybe she wouldn't have to spend as much time in what she considered the place of broken souls. A place where row after row of headstones were all neatly lined up, serving as a reminder of lost lives and the misery for those left behind. She'd never really been a fan of cemeteries, and after her mother passed away, the negative vibes had only increased.

"Not exactly. More like the fact that the cemetery is twice as large as the one at First Congressional, which leads me to believe there are twice as many people buried there. And it's where I went to church when I was younger."

"Very scientific of you, Antique Man." You never knew when he was serious, and when he was kidding—the line between the two almost imaginary. And the more time she spent with him, the more comfortable she became with not knowing. It was all part of the fun. "Why younger? Where do you go now?"

"I haven't been in a while." He shrugged. "Just don't make the time, I guess."

"You should make the time. It's a great place to meet nice people. People who might even share your love of history. People to connect with for more meaningful relationships."

"I never thought about it that way. Honestly, it was something I had to do as a kid, and it went away as adult."

"You should check it out again. You might be surprised by the outpouring of love and connections you can make there."

Blake nodded but said nothing.

"What's our game plan?" she asked, breaking the awkward silence.

"Father Monroe has been around a long time. He'll know what ledgers exist and can help us narrow our search. The town wasn't that big then, so there can't be too many journals to look through—at least I'm hoping. People were religious, and with any luck we'll find a baptism record and a name to go with it."

"Sounds like a good idea." They walked up the steps, the ornate building with its solid wood beams and scrolling wood designs hinting at the history behind its walls.

Sarah had always loved Catholic churches—the stained-glass, beautiful statues, and intricate woodwork timeless pieces of beauty.

Blake pulled the heavy door open and waited for her to enter. An older man walked down the center aisle toward them, sixtyish or so, his gray hair a dead giveaway to his advancing years. His kind smile deepened when Blake stepped around her and reached out to shake his hand.

"Hey, Blake, don't see you here very often. To what do I owe the pleasure? And who's your friend?" His curious gaze never left her face as he asked the questions. Maybe they didn't have many strangers stop in on a Saturday.

"It's great to see you again, Father Monroe. This is my friend, Sarah Dalton. We met at the library and discovered we were researching similar historical information. We've teamed up to help each other and our findings led us here as the next logical step."

"Is that what you young folk call dating nowadays? Research?" He chuckled, the lines on his face becoming deep grooves.

"No. To my knowledge it's still called dating—which we are not. This is called working together."

"I see." Father Monroe's disbelieving glance said the opposite.

"It's nice to meet you." Sarah stepped forward and shook his hand.

"Likewise, my dear. Don't let this young man shortchange you in the courting process." He winked. "Now, why don't you tell me what you're after and I'll see what I can do to help?"

Blake's slight shake of the head was enough of a warning to let the matter drop.

"We're interested in finding the name of the daughters of Owen Westerly. He was a big-time logger and operated a sawmill in Cedar Grove in the early 1800s. He died in 1813 and was survived by two daughters. One of them we know, or at least we're fairly certain, had a name that started with an C. We'd like to check the baptismal records from when the church was first built until around 1800. Do you think they might exist?"

"The church has been lucky enough to have kept all the old records, and although some have been damaged or are yellowed with age, they exist. The original church was built in 1755, although it was a lot smaller than this. Why are you limiting your search to the early 1800s? If the daughter were an infant when he died, it would certainly expand your scope of reference."

"The daughter we're looking for would've been old enough to pen a note to a man in his early thirties. It's a guess on our part and we can expand the range later if necessary."

Father Monroe shook his head. "A young girl under the age of eighteen would have never been allowed to send a man a note. It would be considered improper and if they were a prominent family in the area, the daughter would have been quite protected from dalliances with men. I agree, it should narrow your search. Follow me."

He led them down a short hall, turning right into his office. "Have you checked yet at the First United?"

"No. We thought we'd start here since this church is bigger." Blake spoke from behind her.

Father Monroe indicated for them to have a seat at his desk with a wave of his hand before crossing the room to a metal cabinet.

He pulled a keyring out of his pocket, unlocked the door, and opened it. She could see volume after volume lined up on the shelves inside.

There was something about a record of one's existence that appealed to her, something she hadn't thought of before. People's names were recorded in this town as though they mattered. It gave her a new perspective on the history Blake loved, perhaps for the first time beginning to understand his love for the past. History represented a connection.

Father Monroe pulled the first volume, the gentleness with which he held it a reflection of his deep appreciation for the historical value and it reminded her of Blake.

"I'm sure I don't need to say this, but please be careful. Treasures such as this hold infinite wisdom about the lives of all who came before us and have passed through our doors, people bound together by their love for God and love for one an-other." He handed the book to Blake.

"No worries, Father Monroe. You know me and history." Blake smiled to reassure the older man.

"I do, which is exactly why I'm letting you have access to the books." Father Monroe left the office, leaving the door open as he did.

"Do you think he left it open because he doesn't trust us?" Sarah whispered after his footsteps faded away.

"More likely, he doesn't trust me be-hind closed doors with you. Protocol and all," Blake said, grinning as he leaned in to bump her shoulder. Bound together in their search, his teasing left her off kilter.

"Is this from personal knowledge that he thinks you're a flirt?"

"No. It's probably because he knows no man could resist your freckles." He reached up to brush the back of his hand against her cheek.

It had been a long time since she'd feel this cherished—long enough to make her think twice, at least until her sanity returned. "Flattery will get you most places, but it won't get you out of looking through the journal."

An hour later, Father Monroe stuck his head in the door. "Any luck?"

Blake put his finger on the page to hold their place. "Not yet. You were right about the age and fading, and the writing style is generous in its scrolling curves, so it's hard to make out the letters."

"It's a much more romantic style than the harsh block letters of today. It was during a time when people enjoyed writing the written word. No fancy computers. Let me know if you need anything." He shuffled off, leaving them alone again.

"Hey, look. I found it!" Sarah pointed at the entry, the name Westerly clear and legible. "March 14, 1791. Chloe Westerly, daughter of Owen Westerly and Mary Johnson

Westerly, baptized." Sarah stood to stretch, unable to stop smiling or keep the excitement from her voice. CW was Chloe Westerly. Another piece of the puzzle solved.

"Not so fast." Blake shook his head. "You're not going to believe this."

She didn't like the tone of his voice and moved closer, her hand landing on his shoulder as she leaned over him to see what he'd found.

"March 14, 1791. Claire Westerly, daughter of Owen Westerly and Mary Johnson Westerly, baptized."

"But that's the same day. You've got to be kidding me. Twins?" Just when she thought she was getting somewhere; it went complicated again. Sarah let out a deep sigh.

"There is a good side to this piece of news."

"And what's that, pray tell?" Antique man was always upbeat, but it was easier for him because this news wasn't a huge setback to his own research. Although she wasn't being fair, considering he was spending all his time off helping her.

"For starters, we picked the right church. They were born and raised in Cedar Grove and there's a good chance they're buried here. I think we should check the cemetery and see if we can find out when they died."

"A trip to the cemetery isn't my idea of a fun time, but if it'll save us hours and hours of sitting down behind those horrible, hard-to-read microreaders, I'm all for it."

"There's not much we can do tonight; it'll be dark soon. What do you say to me showing you a good time tonight on the town since you owe me a dinner date? We can poke around the cemetery in the morning when everyone's in church."

"I don't know. The last time a guy tried to show me a good time, he drank too much and forgot which woman he was on a date with. Maybe we should stick with a dinner." Then, of course, there was her ex. A different kind of selfish breed that didn't require alcohol to spur on a wandering eye.

"I guess you need a new memory of what a good time means. Cedar Grove style."

"Why not? You seem harmless, unless of course I should pay attention to Father Monroe's warning."

Their eyes met and held. This close, his eyes were warm and inviting pools of chocolate, magnified by his glasses. His long black lashes were as perfect as any male model on the cover of a magazine. Picture perfect.

"None of those shenanigans in my office or in my church. I take it you two found what you wanted?" They jumped apart.

"We did." Blake found his voice first, saving her from having to answer as she tried to regroup.

"Get out of here and take her on a proper date. You young folks don't know how it's done anymore. After she's all gussied up, you take her to dinner—and no monkey business. Not until you put a ring on her finger and walk her down the aisle. That's how a real gentleman courts a woman if you ask me."

"Yes, sir." Blake's conspiratorial wink as they came around the desk, linked her to him on a deeper level—partners in crime so to speak.

She couldn't help but fast forward to her date with Blake tonight and wonder if he'd kiss her goodnight again—and not on the cheek.

Sarah spent the past hour trying on her limited wardrobe fourteen different ways, searching for the perfect combination. She hadn't been this nervous in forever. It was a night on the town, but he'd called it a date. And with that came the undefined hopes and expectations any woman would have for a night on the town.

Technically, this was their second date, if you counted pizza in the dusty attic. It would sound boring if she repeated the way the evening had gone to anyway else, at least until the kiss. That changed everything, but to what, was still in question. The romance writer in her saw possibilities, but the realist in her knew fanciful wishes did not make it a fact. Wednesday would come all too soon, and she'd be gone.

Blake knocked on her door sharply at six.

"Coming," she hollered. She spritzed on a dash of her favorite lavender scented perfume. Sweet and simple, the scent reminded her of her mother and happier years when the two of them dressed up to go out together, before Sarah had lost her to cancer. She pushed the thought aside and pulled open the door.

Her heart skipped a beat.

Gone were the khaki's and white button-down cotton shirt, and in their place, Blake wore a cream-colored sweater covered by a blue sport coat, matched with blue jeans and cowboy boots. There was nothing geeky about the Blake standing at her door.

"You look stunning." He leaned forward and dropped a kiss on her mouth. Soft and warm, he lingered for a second.

Turns out she didn't have to wait for the end of the date to find out if he'd kiss her. The man was certainly spontaneous, something else she like about him. It kept things interesting.

She took a deep breath, breathing in the spicy cologne he wore. As if on autopilot, one hand landed on his chest. "You look pretty good yourself." The words came out right, but she didn't recognize the flirty tone of her voice. "I seem to remember I was promised a good time, and so far, we are just standing here."

"Sounds like a challenge. I'll have to see if I can improve your image of me over dinner and on the dance floor. I've been known to cut a few good moves." He'd told her they were going to have fun, but he hadn't mentioned dancing. The night kept improving with each minute.

"I hope that doesn't mean you think you're the next John Travolta. That kind of dancing is out of style and would bring your level of refined flair down a notch or two. Or three."

"You'll have to see for yourself. Shall we?" He offered his arm to help her down the stairs. "I made reservations at the Garden Delight, if you don't mind."

"I would've thought he'd be booked solid in advance for a Saturday evening."

"They were, but Jason goes out of his way for his close friends. Lucky for me, I count as one. Right this way, milady."

"You're not dressed for the part. You would need your hair puffed up in curls, a blue velvet jacket and matching pantaloons, white stockings and shiny, pointed shoes. I don't think you're cut out for the 1800s."

He stopped at the bottom of the stairs and smiled. "That's good because I prefer to be in the year 2021."

"Why's that?"

"Because that's where you are." A warm flush of pleasure raced through her. This guy had all the right lines, and as crazy as it seemed, they didn't feel like lines.

And for the first time in a long time, Sarah let her guard down. All the way. For the first time she couldn't help but wonder what could happen after Wednesday.

The possibilities were tempting. Blake was different and inexplicably, she trusted him. Not that he'd said a thing about seeing her again, but maybe tonight he'd suggest it. And if he did, she needed to have an answer ready—one she could live with.

"Good evening, Kyle." Sarah waved but didn't stop to chat since he was checking in new guests.

Kyle waved back and smiled. They continued down the hall toward the restaurant and waited by the podium a minute or two before Jason spotted them and crossed the room, a welcoming smile on his face. "Good evening. It's nice to see you both."

"It's great to see you, too." Sarah loved the warm friendly atmosphere all around her. People in small towns were close knit and even as a stranger in their midst, she felt welcome.

"Blake, I have the table you requested ready."

"Thanks for working with me." Blake clapped Jason on the shoulder good-naturedly.

"Not a problem. Considering this is the first time you've brought a date, it's the least I could do." Jason shook his head and laughed.

"You've got to be kidding. I would've thought this would be his Saturday night special." Sarah didn't believe a word of it. This had to be some guy code kind of thing to make a woman feel like she was different.

Jason eyed her with interest. "Hardly. I think tonight, you *are* the Saturday night special."

"That's enough. Must you give all my boring details?" Shaking his head, Blake looked embarrassed.

"Nothing boring about it. I think it's sweet. And telling." Sarah couldn't help the flush of pleasure warming her. Jason's words led her to believe she and Blake were on the same page and that before she left town, there was a very good chance they'd have *the talk*.

"Follow me." Jason led them past all the tables and continued out the back door. Darkness had settled outside, the cool air a little more than she'd come dressed for.

"I thought we were eating here."

"You are. I don't open the outdoor patio until after Memorial Day, but Blake convinced me to let you two have a private table out here since I'm booked solid tonight." Jason stepped back and gestured with his hand for them to go ahead.

She hadn't seen the table in the corner until she stepped around him.

It was gorgeous. A private dinner for two had been set up under the starry sky, complete with piano jazz music, candles, and a bottle of wine chilling in a carafe. Tea lights lit the garden around the table and the kerosene heater placed nearby was guaranteed to ward off the chill of the evening air while they ate.

It was the most romantic thing anyone had done for her. For a geeky history professor, this guy was a Don Juan when it came to romance. "I love it. You did all this for me?"

"Absolutely. You're worth it." He moved to pull out a chair for her, draping her napkin across her lap after she sat.

"This was all his idea. I have a couple of specials on the menu, but Blake seemed to think he knew which one you'd like and put in your order. Your hors d'oeuvres will be ready in a few minutes." Jason poured wine into their glasses as he spoke.

"It sounds perfect. Thank you." A little high-handed on Blake's part, but she'd trust his judgment, the same way she was coming to trust him.

Blake took a sip of wine. "Very crisp. Nice."

"It's a Sauvignon Blanc, the perfect pairing for tonight's special." Jason placed the bottle in the chiller.

"What did he order? I'm curious."

"The special is a Halibut Piccata with a Lemon Caper sauce and fresh baby artichokes, all served on a bed of quinoa."

"Sounds delicious."

"Great. I'll leave you two alone." Jason headed inside.

"I didn't mean to be overbearing by ordering, but I know you eat shrimp. I thought it worth the gamble since it required advance ordering because of the length of time it takes to prepare. You can say no and order off the menu if you prefer."

In other words, order something else and he'd be eating Halibut again for dinner another night this week. His generosity and concern were flattering. "I meant what I said. It does sound delicious. I absolutely prefer your choice."

"A woman who agrees with me. Wow! I may have to keep you around." His grin was a dead giveaway he was teasing this time. But when he reached out and took her hand, his thumb rubbing gently over her skin, all the teasing vanished.

"And maybe I'll let you." She returned the smile, hoping he understood she meant every word.

"Maybe? What if I tell you there's fresh Strawberry-Rhubarb pie for dessert?" Blake leaned forward, as if her answer was the most important thing in the world.

"My favorite. I think you've discovered the secret to a woman's heart."

"Her stomach? I thought it was a man's heart you reach with food?"

"This is the 21st century. Equal rights." Sarah shook her head and laughed.

"I like it. A modern-day woman exploring the 19th century with me. Life doesn't get any better." He raised her hand and kissed the back of it, letting go when Jason arrived with their appetizer.

Dinner flew by as they exchanged stories and got to know each other. There had to be something wrong with this guy because nobody was perfect, but she had yet to discover it.

Maybe it was time to check out his apartment. Maybe he didn't do his laundry, or like to do dishes, or like to clean. Maybe he left his clothes lying on the floor, dropping them right where he took them off. Not that she wanted him to have flaws, but the deeper she got into whatever this was, the more she wanted to know the real him. No surprises.

Blake paid the bill and took her by the hand, leading her through the restaurant and into the cool evening air. He took off his jacket and wrapped it around her shoulders.

"Thank you. The outdoor heater kept me warm at the restaurant. I need one of those for my patio. But you must be cold," Sarah offered, worried his generosity would backfire.

"I'm alright." He slid his arm around her shoulder. "Now, you have no reason to feel guilty. Close to you, I'll stay warm."

"Another pickup line. How many times have you used that one?"

"Just once. On you." It was no more than the answer she expected and one she fully believed. "We're not going far, just over to the tavern. We can shoot darts, play pool, and dance to an old jukebox that plays in the corner. The Cades Tavern has it all."

"I stopped in there the first night I was here. Nice place."

"I reckon I can pick a song or two you'll like, and maybe even talk you into a slow dance."

"You don't let up, do you? And yes, I'm thinking there's a slow dance or two on my card tonight. I'll have to pencil you in."

"See that you do. And while you're at it, make sure my name's the only name on your dance card."

"Deal." This was going to be a better than fantastic night.

Hours later her feet ached from dancing, but her heart was light and filled with joy. Dance after dance, Blake proved not only his finesse on the dance floor, but his ability to remain attentive to her. Something she hadn't experienced in a long time. Too long. Sarah couldn't help but like the way it made her feel. Special.

She leaned across the table, one hand on his arm. "It's getting late and we both have to work tomorrow."

"True. I'm glad we did this." They walked back to the inn, Blake's hand possessively at the small of her back. No one was at the front desk and they ascended the stairs towards her room.

"You don't have to see me to my door."

"Of course, I do. It was an official date." He smiled and pulled her close as they stood in front of her door.

Mere seconds passed before he leaned down and captured her mouth with a gentle tenderness she found endearing.

"I've got to go." He caressed the side of the cheek and dropped one last kiss on the tip of her nose. Blake stepped back and turned to leave.

"I'll see you in the morning then. Goodnight, and thanks." She watched him head back down the stairs, her thoughts about him more than a little confusing. Sarah had a life in New York, not here. Letting herself start to care about Blake would be a huge mistake. A mistake it would seem she'd already made judging by the way her heart raced.

A mistake Blake hadn't made by the looks of things. Not once had he brought up her ever-looming Wednesday check out from the Crestfield Inn.

Chapter Eight

♥

LAST NIGHT IT HAD been difficult not to push for more of a commitment going forward with Sarah, but the last thing he wanted to do was muddy the waters. It was hard to believe in the matter of three days he felt completely comfortable with her—like they were old friends, but he wanted more than just friendship. It's not like she lived far away, and although not ideal, doable.

Giving her more time to figure out what she wanted to do going forward seemed like a promising idea last night. In the morning light, he wasn't so sure. Nothing would come from holding back and Sarah was putting himself out there.

The crisp morning air put a little extra speed in his steps as he made his way toward the inn, but Blake suspected some of the speed was attributed to the woman waiting for him.

Even if it was a date at the cemetery.

After his last relationship, he'd begun to wonder if there was such a thing as one true love, but in the blink of a nano second in history, he started to wonder if Sarah might be the one.

"Good morning," he called out to Kyle, who was busy fixing the lobby potpourri bowl.

"Good morning. You here to pick up Sarah? You two are getting mighty close."

"We're working together." Blake grinned and started up the stairs. He might hope for more, but Perry wasn't going to be the first to know his feelings.

"That's what they all say. What's on today's agenda? Going to church this morning and then perhaps a picnic lunch in the park, all in the name of business, of course?" Kyle was a young romantic at heart and never missed a chance to push forward his happily-ever-after ideals, especially since he started dating Rachael, one of the seniors at Rushton High.

Blake shook his head and grinned. "You're partially right in a roundabout sort of way. We're headed to the cemetery."

Kyle scrunched his face. "Did you miss Dating 101? You're supposed to make the girl laugh and fall in love with you, not cry and be bored to tears." Kyle shook his head, his lips pursed.

It wasn't his idea of a great date either, but circumstances prevailed over romantic notions. "I'm not trying to make her fall in love with me." Maybe just a little. "I'm helping her do research. Big difference."

"Whatever you say. I've seen the way you look at her. Promise me you'll take her somewhere afterward, someplace better suited to romance."

Why did everyone think he was clueless when it came to his romancing skills? He might not date a lot, but it wasn't his first time out, not to mention, he'd already kissed her. Just because he didn't brag about it, didn't mean it hadn't happened.

Blake climbed the stairs and knocked on Sarah's door.

Dressed in blue jeans and a lime-green cable knit sweater, she looked fresh and ready to go, her hair pulled into a ponytail. "Good morning. I'm glad you put on sneakers. We'll be treading on hallowed ground and we don't want to stir up any ghosts." He laughed, dropping a kiss on her cheek.

"Good morning to you, too. And I'm not sure there's going to be any ghosts at the cemetery—I think they're all here at the inn. Either that, or there's one who has decided to target me for goodness knows what." She wasn't laughing

"What happened last night?" It would be better not to tease her until he found out more.

"Nothing really, I guess. I think it was a dream. All this mucking about in history books and all the pictures, it's giving me an overactive imagination. Last night, I dreamed a woman was dancing around this bedroom. She wore a gorgeous yellow taffeta dress, drawn up tight above her waist with a white ribbon that behind her and flowed down the back. The neckline was lined with delicate lace, and her hair piled high with a matching bow.

"If only you could have seen it. The detail was incredible. She was both elegant and beautiful. She was dancing with a handsome naval officer, pure joy on her face. After the dance, she stood against the wall and watched the others dancing, a wistful expression on her face. It was sad, like the evening didn't turn out the way she wanted. My stories end happily-ever-after, so I know it wasn't me controlling the dream." Sarah let out a deep sigh.

Gone was the smiling, always cheerful woman he'd come to know. This ghost, whether real or imaginary, was starting to get to her. "I'm sure you're right and it's all the pictures we've been seeing in the Gazette. When you write the story of Captain Tremont, you can write the ending anyway you choose. So, make it a happy ending."

"True. But I can't help but feel connected to the woman. I wanted to reach out and comfort her, but she was always out of reach. None of this makes sense. And it's not like I can change anything that happened in the 1800s. Why me?"

"No, you can't. You can, however, embrace the past and the trials the people faced. History matters. People matter. And bringing the two together helps to explain the evolution of progress to our modern-day world."

"Is that why you love history? Because it adds meaning to people's existence and the part they played in making our world what it is today."

"Exactly. Everyone has a story—even your dream lady last night. I love escaping into the past and trying to picture what it was like to live then. Speaking of, are you ready to explore the land of the dead and learn more secrets?" He grinned, hoping a little teasing would ease her tension.

"Not really, but let's go. I'll trust you to keep me safe from ghouls and goblins."

"I promise, milady." Hand in hand, they walked two blocks to the church. Cars filled the parking lot, the guests filing through the big double-door entrance for Sunday morning services.

"Any chance we stop in for the service before we go to the cemetery? The church bells are charming and peaceful. I could use some of the joy one feels when connected to God to help settle my nerves."

"We could, but we don't have much time to explore the cemetery. Maybe another Sunday, if I can convince you to come back to Cedar Grove?" He hung the invitation out there, testing the waters to see where he stood.

Sarah smiled and shrugged. "We shall see."

It wasn't much of a commitment, but at least it wasn't a flat no. Blake took her hand and led her around the building to the back, passing through the wrought iron gates that led to the cemetery. As far as the eye could see, stone after stone represented over two hundred years of Cedar Grove history.

"In case you haven't picked up on my reticence to be here, cemeteries are not my favorite place. If you don't mind, I'd like to stay close together. Maybe if we took two rows at a time and walked at the same pace to examine the headstones, I wouldn't feel alone." She was serious, and it took him by surprise.

He squeezed her hand in understanding. "You'll be all right. I'm not going anywhere, and I promise to fight off any ghosts who try to mess with you." Blake chucked her under the chin and smiled, trying to ease her fears.

"I'll hold you to that promise." Blake would ask her another time about why cemeteries made her uncomfortable, but for now, he'd let it go and give her the support she needed.

They stopped at each grave to investigate the markings. Some of the writing had worn off the stones over the years, making them difficult to read. Some headstones were cracked or broken. Others were basic name plates. And there were larger, more decorative markers—typically in better shape. But it didn't matter if you're rich or poor, the church hadn't differentiated where you were laid to rest. The quality of the headstone was the best indicator they had to judge the status of a grave's occupant.

"Hey, didn't you read Owen Westerly was a big logger and sawmill owner?"

"Yes, why?"

"As a prominent family in town, it stands to reason they would have one of these nicer headstones. If we find Owen's grave, the daughters might be close by because family plots are typically reserved nearby."

"Great idea. Anything that gets us out of here sooner, I'm in." Sarah wrapped her arms around her midsection and rubbed her upper arms vigorously.

"Are you cold?"

"No. I'm fine. It's just . . . the place gives me the creeps."

"We can leave if you need to. Or I can keep checking and meet you at the inn."

"No. It's okay. Cemeteries aren't happy places, but I can do this."

They continued their search, spending less time trying to decipher the small headstones. Blake noticed the empty parking lot, a clear signal they'd been there for hours and whether they found anything or not, it was about time for a break. "We've almost covered this entire place. We must have missed something. He has to be here." She might not want to be in the cemetery, but it hadn't affected her determination.

Blake stopped walking. "That might not be necessary. Come look what I found."

Sarah eased between the graves, being respectful of where she stepped. Blake's admiration rose another notch. He held out his hand when she came to stand near him.

"You found him. Owen Westerly." She threw her arms around his neck and hugged him before turning to the headstone. He liked her enthusiasm.

"Born 1767. Died June 10, 1813. *Respected father and friend.* Sounds like he was a good guy."

Sarah stepped to the right and pointed at the next granite marker. "And look—Chloe

Westerly is buried next to him. Born 1791. Died July 8th, 1815. She was twenty-four. How awful." Sarah shook her head, her shoulders drooping as she let out a deep breath of air. The weight of history and the revelation of Chloe Westerly's early death clearly affecting her.

Blake glanced over at the next stone. "You'll like this even less. Claire Westerly. Born 1791. Died January 5, 1816. That's six months later."

"Wow, talk about tragic." She came to stand next to him, looping her arm in his.

Blake moved his arm, placing it behind her, and drawing her close against him, offering the warmth and comfort she needed.

"It is. But it's things like this that make me want to know the story. To understand what happened, almost to add importance and meaning to their existence." He kissed the top of her head. It was better to keep her grounded in the present, at least until they got out of this place.

"I understand. This isn't just about the note. I'm forging a connection with these women and the challenges they faced in the past—it makes them almost real."

"Exactly." Blake pulled out his phone and snapped a picture of each of the gravesites.

"I'll forward these to you. I've got to teach in the morning, but you might find the cause of death and perhaps more of the story if you look for the obituary in the *Gazette*. And I'll come over after school to help if you come up empty-handed."

"I hope you're right. You do realize we could have avoided this entire expedition of walking through the dead had I stuck with the *Gazette*."

"There was no way to know they met with such tragic deaths. They could have lived to be a hundred for all you know."

"True. There must be a way to find which sister wrote the note, although the why, we may never figure out. It could have been either one. Thank you for sharing this with me. And thank you for protecting me." He took her hand and they left the gloominess of the cemetery behind.

"We make a good team and all we can do is try." It gave her more reason to spend time with him, although he was beginning to hope this thing between them was larger than the project they were working on. When she left in a few days, he wanted to see her again and that required her to feel the same way.

"Any chance I can convince you to go on a picnic with me since we're done? There's not much else we can do until the library reopens tomorrow morning at eight."

She pointed at the sky. "Not such a good plan with those clouds rolling in. How would you feel if I melted?" The sweet sound of her laughter filled the air. Gone was the somberness of the cemetery. It was a welcome change of pace.

"There's not a wicked bone in your body. But you're right about the rain. You could come to my apartment and I'll cook dinner?" The place wasn't ready for a woman's inspection, much less a woman he wanted to impress—but the offer slipped out before he thought much about it. It wasn't that he was a slob, but digging into anything history related, whether on TV or in a book, took precedent over cleaning.

"Or, you can bring a picnic basket to my room at the inn. We can pretend we're on a date in the 1800s. And we can leave the door open. My room overlooks the gardens and it's the perfect spot. What do you say? Are you up for a little fun, antique man?"

The name had grown on him, especially when it came accompanied by her sweet smile. "You're on." And he didn't have to go clean his place. It was a double win for him.

As to pretending they were on a date in the 1800s—if he hadn't been crazy about her already, this would have sealed his interest.

It was a grand idea and one he was prepared to jump right in and do in style. Not to mention, he had the perfect props to pull it off. She had no idea how far he would go, but by the end of the evening, Blake hoped there would be no question about extending their relationship beyond Wednesday.

There was a lot to do before dinner. When they arrived at the inn, Blake dropped a quick kiss on her lips. "See you at six."

"You're not coming in?" Her surprise almost changed his mind about leaving, but not quite.

"I have a date to prepare for." He chuckled, unable to keep from grinning. With a wink, he turned and left her standing on the steps of the inn.

He arrived at his apartment and began to pull boxes from his closet. The black marker writing on the side of one of the boxes meant he found what he was after. *Costumes.*

Right at the top of the box was the outfit he'd worn for the high school play of Pride and Prejudice. It had been a teacher-student event, Blake playing the part of Mr. Bennett. It hadn't been hard for the students to convince him to join in the fun because of his love for history.

He called Jason to discuss what he needed, relieved his friend agreed. All for the price of a little ribbing. Jason intrigued by Blake's interest in Sarah. There would be a picnic basket at the front desk with Kyle when he arrived. With dinner covered, he spent the next hour getting dressed, all while guessing and second guessing his decision to do this.

Sarah hadn't been far off the mark when she once described the dandy she imagined him to be, but instead of blue velvet, she'd have to settle for his dark gold wool tailcoat, complete with braided trim and metallic buttons. Everything else she described was perfect and made to order for their historical date tonight.

Anyone else would've felt the fool walking down the streets of Cedar Grove in the ridiculous looking costume, but not him. It was all in fun, and anytime you could combine history and fun, he was on board.

Kyle doubled over with laughter when he spotted Blake.

"Okay, okay. You've had a good laugh. It's for a good cause. Do you have a picnic basket for me?"

"Don't mind me. I love it. I must say, when I told you to be more romantic, I had no idea what you were capable of. Well done. As to the picnic basket—I believe Jason delivered it to the lady in question." Jason must have misunderstood the plan.

"Thanks. Wish me luck."

"Somehow, I don't think you're going to need it." It was a strange comment, but he'd take it. A vote of confidence was always good.

He knocked on her door, anxious to see her expression when she saw his costume.

She wanted a fun date and he was about to deliver. But when she opened the door, he wasn't sure who was surprised more. Instead of a twenty-first century woman greeting him, a ravishing 1800s Victorian maiden captured his full attention.

Blake swallowed hard. The gown fit her to a tee, emphasizing her figure with its low-cut bodice and high waisted style, the sapphire coloring matching the deep blue of her eyes. Lace, beads, and sequins were intricately patterned on the tippet around her shoulders. Hair piled high on her head, with a bandeau to decorate the tresses, the style revealed her slender neckline and high cheek bones. Simply stunning.

He was glad she hadn't done anything to disguise her freckles. They were the kiss of perfection to her outfit.

Rendered speechless, they simply stared at one another. Seconds later, they both burst into laughter. As she wiped away her tears, Blake remembered the role he was to play for the evening—that of the dashing rake intent on wooing his fair maiden.

Blake wiped the smile from his face and grew serious. He stepped one foot forward, pointed his toe, and placed a hand across his waist—bowing slightly to his lady love. "Miss Sarah, it's a pleasure to behold the sight of your beauty." He straightened and reached for her gloved hand, pressing it to his lips.

"That is most kind of you, Sir Carter. I must say, you are looking rather dashing yourself. Would you care to join me for dinner by the window? Mother says it's okay if I leave the door open. I fear she will be in to check on us fourteen times to make sure all is proper. Cook has prepared a splendid meal." Sarah batted her eyelashes, fanning herself as she peaked past the intricately designed fan with its floral bouquet hand painted across the back.

"I graciously accept your invitation, Miss Sarah. Would your mother not be around,

I would take you in my arms and kiss your ruby lips—but alas, I shall resign myself to thinking of it and shall dream of the day you will allow me the honor." He smiled and leaned in closer, inhaling her fresh lavender fragrance.

"Why, Sir Carter, you flatter me. Mother has gone downstairs and I do believe one small kiss would be in order before she returns." She leaned forward and raised her chin.

Blake's lips twitched into a wide grin, ignoring the temptation of her mouth. "My fair maiden tempts me, but I shall await your mother's permission. I would not be thought a libertine. I fear I want more from you than a stolen kiss."

Sarah played her part like a pro, but the blush on her face couldn't be faked.

"Well then, my good sir, if you would be so kind as to take your seat, we should enjoy the culinary delights of our picnic dinner." She turned and sashayed to the table by the window, her hips swishing the gown from side to side. Sarah lifted the silver cover from the dish and turned to face him. "Come see."

"It smells wonderful—as wonderful as you, my dear." He pulled her chair back. "After you, Miss Sarah." He waved his hand to indicate for her to sit.

"Thank you, Sir Carter." Sarah giggled. She didn't have the benefit of last year's high school play for experience in playing her part, making it difficult to maintain complete decorum. He turned his head away as he walked to take his seat, unable to keep the grin from his face, but not wanting her to see he was having trouble keeping up his role as well.

Blake couldn't remember the last time he'd had this much fun. And the best part about it—it was like this every time they were together. Back-and-forth throughout the meal, they kept up their light banter. When she brought up the twins and the early age at which they died, some of the light-heartedness dissipated. Blake was quick to steer her from the sad subject, wanting the evening to be a success.

The chef had outdone himself with the Coq au Vin Chicken, and Jason had chosen the perfect wine to complete the meal. He'd have to remember to thank him for his part in their evening.

Soft music started to play, the strains of a waltz filling the room. Blake pushed back from the table and stood, crossing to her side. He lifted his hand to her. "May I have this dance, Miss Sarah?"

"I would be most honored to accept." She took his hand and he led her to the middle of the bedroom floor.

Blake kept her at an arm's length away, keeping his frame tight as they danced, light and carefree, almost as if they were one.

One, two, three, four. One, two, three, four. One, two, three, four. One, two—

Sarah stumbled, and Blake wrapped his arms around her, holding her close to keep her from falling—all in the name of safety, of course.

"Did someone suddenly develop two left feet, Miss Sarah?" He grinned, unable to resist teasing her.

"Me, Sir Carter? My good sir, I do believe you are quite mistaken. It was you who had two left feet." She shook her head, disbelief written on her face, her chin rising a notch or two. She had the haughty disdain act down pat.

"I don't think so, but a gentleman never argues with the lady he favors, and I will graciously accept the blame." Decorum forced him to let her go again after the dance—but in that moment, he much preferred the 21st-century. Never letting her go was starting to sound like a grand idea.

Blake's phone rang, intruding into one of the most remarkable nights of his life. And if it hadn't been the ring tone for his mother, he would have ignored it. "I beg your leave, Miss Sarah, tis my mother and I must answer."

"Stop with our fun and answer the phone." She laughed, shaking her head. He watched as she returned to the table and started to clean up while he answered the phone.

"I'm sorry. My mother has fallen and thinks she may have twisted her ankle. I need to run her to the clinic." The call brought a disappointing end to a fabulous night and he still hadn't asked her about seeing him again after she left Wednesday.

"I hope she's okay. Oh, and have fun explaining the costume." Sarah laughed as she pushed him out the door.

"I'll tell her the truth—she'll never believe me. See you after school." Blake dropped a quick kiss on her mouth, regretting he couldn't stay for more.

Chloe frowned. For heaven's sake—barely a kiss goodnight. These two might be dressed for the 1800s, but Sarah lacked some of the more coquettish skills a young lady learned to tempt a man she liked into declaring himself. And Chloe had no doubt Sarah liked Blake and that he, returned the sentiment. But they both were holding out against the inevitable. No dashing rake worth his reputation would have resisted either opportunity to kiss the girl thoroughly, and yet Blake had done exactly that.

Sarah's trip had been no accident—but short of a helping push to put the two together, there wasn't much else Chloe could do. And listening to the two talk at dinner had given her much to think about. It had been heartbreaking to learn of her sister's death shortly after her own. She hadn't seen her since she ran away, Claire having chosen a man over her own twin sister.

Chloe had lost the two people she'd loved most in the world in a single evening, leaving her broken-hearted for what felt like an eternity. Two hundred and four years to be exact.

Throughout the meal she'd listened, hoping to gather more information. Claire's death didn't change what Chloe needed to do. She pushed the sad thoughts away, determined to stay focused on Sarah and finding a way to lead the young woman back in the attic—a place where answers were locked away. Answers that needed to see the light of day. And answers that would free Chloe once and for all.

And while she was at it, she would do her best to make these two recognize their love for each other. Having seen them together a few times, Chloe recognized the truth, having experienced it before in her own life. Although in her case it had been unfortunate Captain Tremont only had eyes for her twin sister.

Chapter Nine

❤

Sarah quickly dressed the following morning, eager to head to the library and look up information on the twins. She wished Blake could be there with her, but the real world was crowding in on their time together.

The date with Blake had been incredible. What had started as a quirky idea for a little fun had turned in to by far, one of the best nights she ever remembered. The only downside was that he hadn't brought up the subject of her coming back to Cedar Grove again. Although to be fair, the evening was cut short.

She could bring it up casually to see if he'd been serious yesterday morning. Nope. She was a modern-day woman with antiquated dating principles.

It was crazy to realize how much she'd come to care about Blake in a few days, but after last night there was no doubt in her mind she wanted to see where things could go from here. He was everything she wanted in a man, right down to a wonderful sense of humor. There was nothing stuffy about Blake Carter.

"Good morning, Kyle." He smiled and waved—the phone glued to his ear.

She continued down the hall to the Garden Delight Café. "Good morning, Jason."

"Good morning. Judging by the twinkle in your eyes and your extra light step, I trust you had a great evening." It hadn't been her imagination; she did look different this morning. "You could say that. And I owe most of it to you." Sarah smiled, walking beside him as he led her to a table.

"What do you mean?" He pulled a chair out for her to sit, placing the napkin in her lap.

"Your picnic basket was a huge hit. I can't thank you enough for putting it together for us on short notice. And the music was a wonderful touch. I didn't know you had speakers in the rooms to pipe in music. After all our research, it was a much-needed break. And you should have seen Blake's outfit—it was almost as if you'd tipped him off you were lending me a gown from the attic. Did you?" She searched his face for the truth, not that it mattered.

"I didn't tip him off, I promise. I wish I'd been here to see it. But I'm not sure what you mean about the music. There aren't any speakers in the guest rooms." He filled her coffee cup.

"There was definitely music. We waltzed like we were at a ball. I'm jealous of the fun the ladies had then, a dashing gentleman to whisk them around the room, doting on their every wish and whim. A girl could get spoiled with that kind of attention."

"I had nothing to do with the music. If neither you nor Blake played it, the only other explanation is that one of guests or our resident ghost had something to do with it. Bettina Crestfield mentioned several stories that included people hearing music, although I never have."

"Based on other things that have happened, it would seem a distinct possibility."

"Will Blake be joining you this morning?"

"No. He's teaching."

Jason picked up the extra place setting. "I'm glad you had a wonderful time. I've got a sausage, egg, and cheese baked casserole and a fresh fruit plate this morning for breakfast. Would you like apple juice or orange juice this morning with your coffee?"

"Orange, please. Thanks. You've done a beautiful job with the inn, right down to every detail. I can't begin to tell you how much I'm enjoying my visit here.""

"Thank you. Before I moved to Cedar Grove, I was in architectural design. Good money, but it didn't allow me the freedom to enjoy my creations. It's why I love the inn and have poured my heart into fixing it up, restoring it to its former glory."

"That's awesome. It's how I feel about my writing. Being happy in what you're doing is more important than fame and fortune."

"Spoken like a true starving artist." He chuckled. "Seriously though, you are right. What's on your agenda this morning now that you've lost your research partner to the school system?"

"We found some information on the Westerly daughters yesterday at the cemetery. It turns out they were twins—Claire and Chloe. Such a tragedy. They died six months apart. Maybe one couldn't live without the other. I'm hoping to find what happened by cross referencing the dates to the microfilm at the library. I've got today and tomorrow to solve the mystery."

His eyebrows arched upward, a questioning gaze on his face. "Nothing in town to entice you to stay longer?" She knew exactly what he meant—not nothing, but no one. *Blake.*

"I have deadlines and must return home as planned. As to coming back, it depends. I live a couple of hours away." Everything between her and Blake was too new to be saying anything, not to mention she was still unsure. The long-distance thing had been a disaster with Larry. And although her ex wasn't nearly the caliber of man Blake was, it didn't keep Sarah from worrying about making another mistake.

"Very little time when it comes to matters of the heart."

"True. Very true."

"I'll have your breakfast out in a moment." Jason left, stopping at another table on the way to the kitchen.

Sarah gazed out the window, once again admiring the garden views. The flowers were starting to blossom as each day brought warmer and warmer temperatures. Spring represented fresh beginnings and had always been a special time to her. After a chilly winter, the warming temperatures and colorful arrays bursting open all around always managed to warm her both inside and out.

She inhaled every bite of the casserole, the cheesy concoction addictive. She finished off her orange juice, grabbed her handbag, and headed for the door. It was time to get down to the business of history.

"I'm off to the library. See you later this afternoon."

Jason waved as he sat another couple for breakfast.

The warm sun beat down on her face. Pulling her sweater tight, she sucked in a breath of fresh morning air, the coolness invigorating. It was a short walk to the library. She reached for the handle of the door and pulled, but nothing happened. She spotted a note taped to the center of the door.

Due to an emergency, the library will be closed until noon.

Disappointed, she turned to leave. With nothing else to do, Sarah decided to explore the town some more, determined to make the best of this tiny setback in her plans.

She stopped at Bixby's for a cup of coffee and a donut after remembering Blake's advice not to miss Katrina's baked pastries. The server had been quick to recommend, quick to chat, and quick to refill her cup, earning her a large tip and Sarah a new friend.

Leaving the diner, she turned right and headed down the street, avoiding the cut through Blake had used. Running into Alicia wasn't high on her priority list. She walked past Kathy's Hair Salon, stopped, and turned back. Why not? The sign said open. She pushed the door open, the tinkling cow bell announcing her arrival. A woman came out from the back hallway, full of smiles. She was stunning, her red hair and green eyes a unique combination.

"Come in. I'm Kathy. How can I help you?"

"Do you have time for a walk in? I was thinking maybe a cut and style, something fresh for spring."

"I have plenty of time. No one scheduled until eleven. Take a seat and tell me what you have in mind. I have some magazines if you'd like to look through them for ideas, and coffee or tea while you do."

"That sounds wonderful. Black coffee sounds nice. Thanks."

It wasn't long before Sarah gave herself over to the woman's soothing touch as she massaged her scalp, her fingers like magic as she washed, rinsed, and conditioned her hair. The soothing warm water lulled Sarah into a place of relaxation. A place where everything else in her life vanished except living in this very moment.

No hurry. No deadline. No nothing. It had been a long time since she'd enjoyed pampering of this sort.

Kathy trimmed her hair and chatted about life in town and people, occasionally coming up for air to find out more about Sarah. She didn't mind one bit because it had always been hard for her to figure out what to talk about to fill the awkward gaps of silence. The foiled highlights took quite a bit of time, but the results were stunning.

Sarah turned her head from side to side, checking the shortened tresses that glimmered back at her in the mirrored reflection. Not too short, but with several inches gone, the hair danced as it moved. Kathy had sheared the front edges, and they curved around the angle of her jaw and framed her face. Fresh and exciting, like spring.

Would Blake notice? The man was into details and she couldn't wait to hear his opinion.

She headed for the library, relieved when she saw the sign had been taken down and found the doors unlocked. "Good afternoon, Perry. Is everything okay? I was worried about you."

"Good morning. It is, and I apologize. I can't remember the last time I didn't open this place on time, but I had a little health issue last night that needed checking this morning. Doc says everything should be fine." The librarian looked worn out.

It was more than the bags under his eyes, it was also the way he carried himself. It might have been better if he'd taken the day off and kept the place closed, even if it had meant she would have had to wait until tomorrow to research the files. "Sorry you had a rough evening, but I'm glad you got good news this morning."

"You headed to the media room? I guess Blake's in class."

"Yes, and yes. You won't believe this. We found out we're dealing with twins, and both died young and within six months of each other. I'm hoping to find a cause of death."

"What a shame. Good luck—old records are hit and miss. If there's anything I can do to help, let me know." Perry looked up as a woman approached, a pile of books in her hands.

"Thanks."

Sarah tossed her things on the table and crossed the room to the filing cabinet. She pulled the file that included 1815 and 1816 and sat down at the reader. Blake had texted her a good-morning wish and the photos of the headstones. She flipped through her phone gallery to recheck the dates.

Advancing the film to the first July 1815 entry, she started scanning each page, looking for the society page in hopes of discovering Chloe's obituary.

Nothing. Her hopes dwindled and she advanced the film to the next week's publication.

And then she saw it.

Chloe Westerly, daughter of the late Owen Westerly, died July 8th, 1815, while staying at the Crestfield Inn. Miss Westerly is reported to have fallen down the stairs after tripping on a rug. Local authorities say Miss Westerly had been dealing with a bout of depression after her twin sister moved away. Services were held at the St. Mary's Catholic Church, where she is buried.

Chloe Westerly died at the inn.

Sarah couldn't have been more shocked. Could Chloe be the presence she felt at the house? And if so, why was she seeking her out? Maybe the ghost knew who she was and was trying to tell her something. It was crazy, but in a way, it made perfect sense to Sarah's over-active imagination.

She could barely contain her excitement as she reached for the microfilm marked 1816 and inserted it into the reader. She started at the beginning, searching the January publications for Claire's obituary. It didn't take long to find, although parts of it were harder to read than others.

Claire Westerly, daughter of Owen Westerly of Cedar Grove, died January 5, 1816, giving birth to her infant son, Caleb. Miss Westerly was staying in Bellevue at the time with a friend. Miss Westerly is buried at St. Mary's Catholic Church cemetery in Cedar Grove, Vermont. The infant son was taken in by Mr. and Mrs. Frank Lawrence, a happy blessing for the couple who had been unable to have children of their own.

A baby? Another surprising turn of events. Sarah's heart ached for these two women. Fate had not been kind.

It had been a blessing the Lawrence family had taken in the infant, yet another example of small-town life and a sense of community. It was a place where people banded together to take care of their own.

Caleb Lawrence. The name rang a bell. Sarah got up to retrieve her notebook. She flipped through her notes. Where had she heard that name before?

Caleb Lawrence—the name underlined and circled. Blake was looking for this man's parents and Sarah had fallen into the information. Frank and Mary Lawrence. She couldn't wait to tell him.

Except the Lawrence's were the adoptive parents.

Claire Westerly was Caleb's birth mother.

No. No. No. Sarah shook her head, trying to drive away the unthinkable thought forming in her head.

It didn't work. Blake Carter was a direct descendent of Caleb Lawrence and therefore of Claire Westerly. CW. It wasn't possible. What were the odds?

She rubbed her forehead, trying to wrap her brain around what she'd discovered. It was crazy to think their searches turned out to be connected, and crazier yet with the newest twist.

She and Blake might be related.

If Claire had a relationship with Captain Tremont and he had fathered a child, both she and Blake were direct descendants of Captain Tremont. She paced the room, trying to process what this would mean.

And she'd kissed him. More than once. And worse, she had feelings for him, and those feelings were far from cousinly. To Sarah, no matter how distant, the very idea seemed unthinkable.

Blake.

One thing for certain in this mess, was until they knew more, their kissing days were over. She couldn't bring herself to go down that road. If they did a DNA test and found they were related, there was no way she could date him. By most people's standards the relationship would be so far in the distant past, they wouldn't consider it a problem, but to Sarah it would be weird. And something she wasn't sure she could handle.

This new twist was more like a huge warning sign she should have never let herself start to care about him. When it came to her and relationships, they never worked.

Sarah sent him a text before she lost her nerve.

We need to talk. Call me when you're done at school.

Chapter Ten

♥

SARAH RETURNED TO THE inn, thankful she hadn't run into anyone. She paced the room, counting down the minutes until he called. The phone rang at five minutes after three, and she wasn't surprised to see Blake's name light up on the screen.

"Hey there, I got your message. What's up?" Based on the urgency in his voice he must have sensed she had news—but there was no way he would come close to guessing.

"I was at..." She closed her eyes. Explanations over the phone didn't feel right, not to mention, there'd be no way to gauge his reaction. "I think we should talk in person.

Maybe we can meet somewhere? Like at the park?" Sarah stopped pacing long enough to wait for his answer.

"*Ummm*. Okay. Is everything all right?" It would be easier to tell him on the phone and get it over with, but it wasn't the right thing to do. A few more minutes wouldn't change anything.

"I'll tell you when I see you. It's a bit crazy is all." Crazy was an understatement. Sarah shook her head, frustrated their research had brought them to a point of no return.

"You're starting to worry me."

"It is what it is. You'll understand when I tell you." She needed to hang up before she took the easy way out and spilled the information.

"I'm on my way. There's a bench to the right when you first enter the park off Main Street. Meet me in five minutes."

"Okay." She disconnected the call and headed out the door.

The five-minute walk felt like an hour, and with each step, her feet grew heavier.

She spotted Blake waiting by the bench, his phone pressed to his ear. He hung up when he noticed her and met her part way. Reaching for her hand, he pulled her close, leaning down to kiss her. Sarah barely managed to turn her head in time, letting his lips land on her cheek.

Blake pulled back, his forehead drawn tight, his gaze piercing her with intensity. "What's wrong? Have I done something to upset you?"

She pulled her hand from his and folded her arms across her chest. "No, it's nothing you've done. I found out some major news today at the library."

"You don't sound very excited."

"Because the information has many variables. Confusing ones. There's no other way to tell you this, so I'm going to come right out and say it. You and I might be related."

She let out a deep breath trying to ground her spinning emotions.

"That's crazy. What makes you think it's a possibility?" Not a hint of the impact of her news crossed his face, at least not that she could tell.

"I found Caleb Lawrence's parents. He was taken in by Frank and Mary Lawrence after his own mother died in childbirth, and I found out his real mother's name."

"That's great. But what does it have to do with us?"

"His mother was Claire Westerly. CW." Sarah waited, giving Blake time to process the information.

He shook his head in disbelief, but she could tell he hadn't put two and two together. "Start from the beginning and tell me what you found. And how you think this affects you and me?" Suddenly, his eyes widened, and his mouth dropped open.

Bingo. It would seem Blake had connected the dots.

"I found out Chloe passed away not long after Captain Tremont, and she died at the Crestfield Inn after falling down the stairs. Such a tragic ending. I wonder if my ghostly visits might be Chloe. What if she's trying to reach the captain for some reason and realizes I'm related to him and here to research what happened the night he died. The big question is—does she want me to know what happened or does she want to keep me from finding out?"

So far, her ghost appeared to be friendly. Sarah was going to stick with that premise unless anything happened to change her mind. It made her more determined to figure out what Chloe wanted her to know.

"This is insane. And how would Chloe tie into anything between Claire and Captain Tremont? You must admit this is pretty far-fetched, not to mention it happened a long time ago."

"I don't know. I've tried to piece it together this afternoon. The article mentions Chloe had been battling with depression after her sister left town, but what if Chloe was upset because the captain died? The twin issue is another problem because based on the timing when Claire left Cedar Grove, she was already pregnant."

"It sounds to me like you're reading and writing too many romance novels." He smiled at her and tried to pull her into his embrace.

"No." She held her ground. "We can't do this. Us. Not until we know the truth. I'm sorry. We might be related, and it just seems weird. Wrong." Her eyes filled with unshed tears as she fought against the emotions crying out for things to be different. Life wasn't fair.

"If what you say is true, it depends on whether Captain Tremont fathered Claire's child." He took a deep breath and sat on the bench. "And it was over two hundred years ago. It shouldn't matter to you and me. We could do a DNA test if it would make you feel better, but for me, this changes nothing. I want to see you again after you leave. Last night, I was going to talk to you about us, but we were interrupted before I got the chance."

"I don't know. For me, it's different. I'm at a loss what to do or where to go from here." She couldn't help the way she felt about the awkwardness of the situation any more than she could control how much she liked Blake. And standing in the middle of the indecision wouldn't help her decide. Only answers could do that.

"It's unbelievable our search led to the same place, but as to the answers, we do what we can to find them, but it doesn't change the way I'm starting to feel about you. I don't want you to go home and forget we ever met," Blake said, a note of desperation in his voice.

He was saying all the things she wanted to hear—before her discovery. "I'm sorry, Blake. I'm not sure I want to pursue anything between us if by chance we're some distant family relation. We would have the same great-grandfather generations ago." It was hard to understand his lack of concern regarding the situation. It wasn't like this was something you came across every day and knew how to handle.

"This is ridiculous, and you know it. Even the laws of society have weighed in on this, and it's acceptable. The strictest of laws says first cousins once removed can't be married. I'm not even sure there is a label for any kind of relationship we might have based on what occurred six generations ago."

"I don't see it the same way you do." And she didn't like that he wasn't trying to see it her way. If they mutually agreed, it would have freed her from the guilt. Instead, he was laying it all at her feet.

"What do you suggest we do?" Blake leaned against the bench, his shoulders tense, his gaze unyielding.

"We know both sisters were staying at the Crestfield Inn and that Claire left before Chloe died. I'm hoping maybe their belongings might have been thrown in a trunk and put in the attic since neither one ever checked out. There's so many antiques and collectibles stored there, and it would make perfect sense. I wanted to ask Jason if I can go through the trunks to see if any of them belong to the Westerly twins, but he was out earlier."

"It's a great idea and I'll help you look. But I stand by what I said; nothing changes for me no matter what we find." His gaze intensified as he waited for her answer.

It's not that her feelings had changed either, but whether to act on those feelings or not had. She wished it didn't matter, but it did. "You have to teach tomorrow."

"I know, but I'm not letting you get rid of me that easy. I'll call in and take a personal day. Besides, I need more time to change your mind."

"Blake…"

"I like your hair by the way—very beauti-ful."

Of course he'd noticed. He was Blake.

Fear of speaking up last night had cost Blake dearly. Now, there was chance he'd lose Sarah before they ever even had a chance. Although, considering her news and her feelings about it, it's not like she wouldn't have put the brakes on a relationship with him anyway.

Something like this wasn't a common oc-currence, and neither of them had experi-ence to draw upon for answers, but it was all ancient history.

Where did you draw the line? More peo-ple would find they were related if they looked far enough back. To him, it was all about two people living in the now. Maybe Sarah was using this as an excuse to pull away? Or maybe she needed time to come to terms with the information. The last thought, wishful thinking on his part. Time he could give her, space on the other hand, not a chance. Not yet, anyway.

"Why don't we stop at Murphy's and grab a couple of subs before we head over to the inn. We only have until nine."

"That would work. I'm sorry, Blake." She reached out to touch his arm, stopping as if she thought better of it.

"Don't worry. We'll figure this out—together." He felt helpless, but for her, he'd be strong.

Thirty minutes later, they were back at the inn and searching for Jason. It didn't take long to locate him and catch him up to date. After Jason gave his blessing and handed over the key, they headed for the attic.

Blake noticed she hadn't pointed out the relationship issue, but it was better left unsaid. The one thing they didn't need at this point was everyone else's opinion on the matter. Two opposing opinions were quite enough.

They climbed the stairs and Blake unlocked the door. He flipped on the lights, taking the bag of food from her and setting their dinner at the table. A sense of déjà vu struck him, having done this with her the second night they met—the same night he discovered a woman who not only intrigued him, but one he wanted to know more about.

After devouring the subs, they went straight to work, systematically starting in one corner of the attic. Conversation during the meal had been stilted and Blake wasn't sure what to do next.

Popping open each trunk, they pulled out the contents, trying to find some way to identify the time period and owner. He noticed goosebumps up and down her arms. "Are you cold?"

"I'm fine. I felt a sudden chill, is all."

"Here, put my jacket on." Blake moved to the table and retrieved his jacket.

"I don't want dust all over it."

"No worries." He draped it over her shoulders, his hands lingering. Her faint smile warmed him. He wanted nothing more than to drop a kiss on her lips, but held back, not wanting to upset her. It wouldn't take much to spook her at this point and he wasn't ready for the evening to end.

"It feels like there's cold air coming in from somewhere. I'll check the windows."

"I feel it too. What about that one?" She pointed to the window in the far corner.

"Everything's closed." He walked over to stand beside her. "Perhaps we should call it a night and resume our search in the morning."

"Okay." Sarah closed the trunk, a cloud of dust billowing around them. Blake offered his hand to help her up. He sneezed as she tried to grab his hand, the motion driving him backwards and out of her reach.

She lost her balance and fell backward, landing against a spinning wheel, which in turn bumped into a school desk, which in turn knocked down the painting standing next to it.

"I'm sorry. Are you okay?" He looped his arm under hers and pulled her to her feet, afraid she might have been hurt in the fall.

"I'm fine. Shhhh." She smiled at him. "If any of the guests complain about the noise, Jason will have our heads."

"More reason for us to leave now." Blake righted the spinning wheel and moved to stand the painting up. He glanced down at the image. Two women stood in front of a vaguely familiar home.

He held the painting to the light, trying to read the inscription. Westerly - 1814. He took a closer look at the women in the painting and realized they were identical.

"Sarah, look. It's the Westerly twins. This must be their old homestead. I know this house. It's on the corner of Tally and Anderson, right here in Cedar Grove.

"The house has changed hands quite a few times that I know of, but the owners have always preserved some of these unique features built by the original owner. The craftsmanship is incredible, which stands to reason since he owned the lumber yard and a sawmill."

Sarah stood next to him admiring the painting. "This is great." She reached out to touch his arm. In her excitement she'd forgotten her reservations, which he took as a good sign.

"It means there could be more of their belongings here."

"Is everything okay?" Jason stood in the doorway, a curious expression on his face.

"Yes, sorry. I was a little clumsy and bumped into something. Sorry if we disturbed anyone. We were getting ready to lock up for the night when Blake found a painting of the Westerly twins."

"That's awesome. Sounds like you're close to solving your puzzle. You two make a good team."

"That's what I keep trying to tell her." Blake gave her a playful nudge. And he would keep on telling her until she listened. *Again.*

"Based on what you two told me earlier tonight, I think you should take the painting, Blake. It sounds like it belongs to you. And anything else you find that belongs to the Westerlys', is yours."

This he hadn't expected or thought of. Westerly blood flowed through his veins, tying him to some of the founders of Cedar Grove. "Thanks, that's a generous offer. This is all so new."

"I'll lock up. I'm sure you two have lots to talk about." He looked from one to the other and back again. Neither spoke, each one unwilling to voice the issue uppermost in their minds.

"Thanks." With the painting in hand, Blake waved goodbye. He led Sarah to her room, said goodnight and left, all without a kiss or a touch. Nothing between them had changed as far as he was concerned, but the painting changed everything else for Blake.

Chloe had the wind knocked out of her ghostly soul. The last thing she expected to hear was that her sister had a son. Caleb. And the heartbreak of learning Claire had died in childbirth was almost too much to bear.

It was hard to remain focused, but she had to, for the captain's sake. And the biggest question at this point was, who was the father? Claire had been wooed by both Captain Tremont and Jack Spry—the soldier her sister had fallen in love with shortly before she met the captain.

Chloe had heard it all. Claire never stopped debating her choice between love and being the captain's wife, and all the things he could pro-

vide her. She'd never wanted for anything again, except the love of her precious Jack. Over and over her sister had bemoaned her dilemma, oblivious to Chloe's feelings for the captain. And unbeknownst to Chloe, her sister had been pregnant when she'd left Crestfield Inn.

At least she finally understood the connection she'd felt whenever Blake came around. He was family. Maybe they would never know the identity of the father, but for Chloe, it didn't matter. Sarah was close to solving the mystery of what happened, and when she did, Chloe would be free from the chains that held her bound to this realm.

Then what? She'd never thought past what would have happen once the wrong had been righted. Crestfield Inn would always be special in her heart, after all, it was there she'd been granted one dance with the captain. A dance engrained in her memory and played over and over. It was the only thing she had of him, aside from her guilt for the part she played in his death.

If she'd left it up to Sarah and Blake, it might have taken those two a week to go through everything. And with Sarah leaving Wednesday, Chloe didn't have that long. Stirring up a little dust to orchestrate a reaction had been a capital idea, and it had worked, much to her credit.

Those two were meant for each other, but something had happened. She couldn't imagine what had changed between last night and now, but Chloe was determined to fix it. Making sure Sarah didn't walk away from Blake was the very least she could do in exchange for the girl's help in righting past wrongs.

Chapter Eleven

♥

Thoughts of Blake flitted in and out each time Sarah rolled over throughout the night, making it almost impossible to sleep. But there was at least one window of time she had to have slept, because it had been enough for her to dream—or be visited. *Again.*

She wasn't sure which twin, but Sarah was positive it was one of the Westerly women, the young woman's image the same as the one in the painting.

This time, the woman wore a plain blue gown of cotton drawn tight around her high waist, with only tiny bows of dark blue around the bodice as embellishment. Hair down, her long tresses tumbled freely as she curtsied to an imaginary partner, dipping low and nodding her head, as if agreeing to dance.

The woman's arms were extended as if she were dancing.

Sarah would have expected a dreamy smile on the woman's face, perhaps recalling the thrill of a joyous moment with her beau as she danced around the room. Instead, there was sadness reflected in her eyes. The music was the same song that had played when she and Blake danced, and the one playing in the first vision she'd had.

At the end of the lyrics, the woman curtsied and walked away. She crossed the room and sat down on an old trunk, a look of sheer misery on her face. And then the woman vanished. The vision was almost the same as the first night she'd seen the woman in her dreams, and yet the differences seemed important. The dress color had changed, the room had changed, and this time, there had been no man.

For hours, Sarah lay awake trying to decipher the meaning. The only explanation she could come up with was that the woman was pretending the second time. Perhaps an unrequited love had caused the woman's sadness.

Today was Sarah's last day in Cedar Grove and her last chance to figure out which Westerly sister sent the note and why, and it was possibly her last day with Blake. She rolled out of bed to dress, knowing he would be here soon. His abrupt departure last night reminded her of the wall she'd erected between them, and although it was for the best, she didn't like it.

Fifteen minutes later, she heard him knock. He greeted her with a warm smile.

"Good morning." He leaned forward but checked himself. "I brought coffee and donuts, unless you prefer to go down to the restaurant and save these for later." A rush of disappointment filled her when he hadn't even bothered with a friendly kiss on the cheek. It was her own fault, and she couldn't complain. He was, after all, only following her stupid rules.

"No, that's fine. We have a lot of territory to cover. I appreciate you taking the day off, although it wasn't necessary." She wasn't ungrateful by any means, but it was awkward given the circumstances of her discovery.

"It was to me." After having the night to mull things over, Blake hadn't changed his mind about her. It gave her an odd, mixed-up sense of relief.

"Jason gave me the key already, so we're good to go."

"We should start where you found the painting. Did you already hang it? It was nice of Jason to give it to you." They made small talk as they climbed the stairs.

"I found the perfect place for it, but I need to run by the hardware store later for the proper anchor screws, so it doesn't pull out of the drywall. Jason's a great guy. I've only known him a little while, but what I know, I like."

The two of them spent the next hour searching for anything belonging to the Westerly twins and talking about almost every subject they could think of, except of course the real issue between them. Only stopping for coffee breaks every now and then, they stayed focused, picking their way through desk after desk, trunk after trunk, and cabinet after cabinet, searching for clues.

Blake stopped and pulled out a chair and sat facing her. "This attic is big, but not big enough for the elephant in the room, and I'm tired of skirting around the issue."

"Blake—"

"Hear me out. You had your say yesterday and now it's my turn. The world we live in is full of people, and somewhere down the line, everyone is related. It's history. And whether it's two hundred years or two thousand years, it shouldn't matter. The history of mankind unites all eventually."

Sarah hadn't thought of it that way. She knew he was right, but she couldn't bring herself to say it didn't matter. To her, it did. They might have the same great-grandfather. Six-times removed.

"The logical side of my brain says you're right, but a part of me finds it awkward. Maybe digging up the past wasn't such a good idea."

"I disagree. If you hadn't been digging into the past, we would've never met. Just because you're leaving tomorrow, doesn't mean I'll give up on us. Thought you should know."

"I wanted to see you again too; you must know that." She took a deep breath. *What was she doing?* Did she want to throw away the best thing that had ever happened in her life?

Maybe it wouldn't work, but she wouldn't know if she didn't try. Coming here, a relationship was the last thing she was looking for, but love had found her anyway. At least, she was sure that's where her feelings were headed before she was forced to put a brake on them.

"Just give me time. Please." She needed time to wrap her head around the truth and figure out if she could live with the results.

"Take as much time as you need. I'm not going anywhere."

Hours passed until the rumbling of Sarah's stomach forced them to acknowledge it was time for a break. They'd managed to cover half the attic—surprisingly good for a morning's work.

"Only half the room to go." Her gaze swept across the other side, taking in each piece of furniture. She tried to calculate the time it would take to finish. Sunlight streamed in from the skylight casting a bright glow in a ray of light across the room, reaching the darkened corner of the attic.

Sarah caught sight of an intricately designed trunk, the patterned brass vaguely familiar. She shrugged it off. After all the time they'd spent looking in the attic, everything started to look the same.

They headed for the door, but she stopped, turning around for one last look. A vision from her dream flashed in her mind. The woman curtsied and sat down on a trunk. She raced over, trying to make sure her eyes and brain weren't tricking her into seeing something that wasn't real. Nothing doing. This was it. "Wait, Blake. I saw this trunk in a vision last night."

"What? You didn't tell me you had another one." He crossed the room and joined her.

Her heart raced as she reached for the buckles. She paused, glancing at him. "When I talked to Jason, I mentioned the music we heard. But he told me there are no speakers in my room and no music is piped throughout the house. The only explanation possible is a ghost."

"I'd say there's probably some other worldly reason, but what does that have to do with this?"

"In my vision, one of the Westerly twins was dancing and the next thing I knew, she sat down and started crying."

"And?"

"The woman sat down on this trunk. I'm sure of it." Sarah pulled at the straps, eager to look inside. Goosebumps raced down her spine knowing she was right about the trunk—and almost certain she was right about Chloe.

"That's crazy. We both know you won't eat a bite until we finish checking this out, so let's get to it. You realize, don't you, that you might have seen the trunk yesterday while we were here."

"Don't be such a disbelieving stick-in-the-mud. I'm sure I'm right."

"Hey, you're the one with the rumbling stomach." He pulled the trunk away from the wall, making room for her to open the lid.

A blue cotton gown with tiny blue bows decorating the bodice lay folded on top, delicately preserved in the cedar chest. "That's it! That's it! It's the gown she wore in my vision last night." Sarah stood and pulled the garment from the trunk, holding it to her chest and twirling about as if she were dancing.

"It would look good on you." He stepped in close and bowed, offering his hand. "Perhaps we are destined to dance again, Miss Sarah."

Sarah couldn't help but laugh. The thought of dancing with Blake made her giddy with excitement, more so than finding the gown or the trunk.

Blake pulled several other dresses from the trunk, laying them across some of the nearby chairs. Beautiful colors filled the attic, the gowns were wrinkled, but otherwise in excellent condition. The delicate lace and fabric spoke of an owner who spared no expense in the wardrobe.

"Stop. I know that yellow gown. It's the one from the first vision. Oh, my gosh. I can't believe it. Chloe is real. It's the only way I would know these dresses and the trunk. This is what she wanted me to find."

"Either that or you have a very active imagination—but then again, you are a writer."

Shivers slid down her spine. It was an incredible find, whether Blake believed her or not. She knew the truth. "I know what I saw—your loss if you don't believe." She shrugged, turning back to reveal the treasures buried deep within the chest.

"I didn't say I didn't believe. Keeping my options open is more like it."

"Look at all this stuff. There're books, pictures, knick-knacks. This is amazing. And here's the ledger from the sawmill and the lumber company and it has a big W embossed on the front. Told you this was it. And look, here's a stack of letters addressed to Claire Westerly. Are you still on the fence, antique man?"

"No comment. Let me see the ledger." She handed it to him, far more eager to check out the letters.

He flipped several pages, a few murmurs and grunts slipping out as he pored over the document. "Interesting."

Sarah stopped opening the letters to look at Blake. "What?"

"These ledgers continue past when Owen Westerly was alive. The twins must've kept the business going, but it looks as though it continued to lose business and profitability at a rapid rate.

"There are several handwritten notes that appear to question the numbers. Makes me wonder what happened all those years ago after their father died. Another mystery, maybe one for another trip down memory lane." He closed the book and stacked it with some of the other items on the nearby table.

She opened one letter after another, scanning the contents. "Look. Here's a letter from Captain Tremont. He writes of his love for Claire and that he can't wait for her to meet his daughter." From the moment she discovered that she and Blake might be related, she'd been on edge. Her heart ached with the reality she had to face. They had proof Captain Tremont and Claire were in love, which pointed even more in the direction that she and Blake were related.

It meant she would need to come to terms with how she felt and decide if she could let their relationship move to the next level. Why did it have to be this way? *Life wasn't fair.*

She opened the next letter. "Here's another one." *Wait. What*? "You won't believe this. It's a love letter from a man by the name of Jack Spry. Seems Claire couldn't make up her mind between suitors." There was a chance they weren't related, and Sarah was more than happy to grasp at each thread of remaining hope.

"She made up her mind enough to sleep with one of them. That would've been no small concession in 1815. For a woman of her station in life, the love motivating her decisions must've been quite strong to go against the bounds of polite society."

"Spoken like a true historian with a heart." He was a romantic whether he wanted to believe it or not.

"Keep reading. Only one of these men can be the father of Caleb Lawrence and for our sake, I hope the answer is in those letters. I meant what I said. I'm not letting you slip away out of my life as fast as you blew into it."

It was easier not to answer. Her stomach rumbled again.

"Why don't I put this stuff away and you bring the rest of the letters to read over lunch?"

She let out a deep sigh and sat back on her heels. She'd come this far, and they were close, but at what price? "Maybe I shouldn't read on. Maybe it will ruin everything."

"It already has, and you won't rest until you've read every word, not only for the captain's sake, but for ours." Blake stopped putting things in the trunk. He leaned forward and slid his hand over the back-left corner.

"What is it? Did you find something else?" Sarah moved closer, peering inside.

"There's something under the lining. I'm sure of it." He peeled back the top layer of fabric to reveal a secret pouch. "Look, another book."

He flipped open the black cover. "It's Chloe Westerly's journal."

Sarah's hands trembled as she took it from him. A cool chill raced down her spine.

"She's with us now. I feel her. *Chloe*."

"This is what she wanted you to find, and it's time to find out why. Read it." Obviously, Blake no longer doubted her about the Westerly ghost.

"I think you're right." Sarah skimmed the pages, unable to believe the heartfelt words poured out into the journal. The story might have been written hundreds of years ago, but the reading of it made it seem like yesterday.

"Chloe was in love with Captain Tremont. It appears we have stumbled into a love triangle."

"That couldn't be good, especially with twins. Can you tell who wrote the note?"

"It was Chloe. She writes in her journal that Claire has run off with Jack Spry. Chloe, it seems, wrote the note and sent it to the captain telling him not to come to the Crestfield Inn because she didn't want him to follow Claire and try to change her mind. She thought with Claire out of the picture, she might have a chance with the captain someday."

"Go on. This is fascinating."

"The love story, the history, or the mystery?" Sarah couldn't help but tease him.

"All three perhaps. Don't keep me in suspense."

"Chloe hoped one day she would have a chance to win the captain's heart with her sister out of the picture. In another entry after the captain's death, she describes finding out the captain had sailed across the lake anyway, his ship capsizing in the storm. She mentions the horrible guilt she felt in causing him to venture out that night.

When she learned he'd been dishonorably dismissed because they thought he was smuggling, she'd been determined to travel to New York to right the wrong committed and have the captain's honor restored. The last entry was dated days before she died."

"It would seem you were right. Perhaps she was depressed about the captain and her sister. It was unfortunate she fell before being able to fix things. Look how many lives were affected by all this."

A cool draft brushed across her skin. This is what Chloe wanted her to find. In her hands, Sarah held irrefutable proof of the captain's honor.

A sense of peacefulness settled around her as if Chloe knew what this discovery would mean. The only secret left unturned was that of the identity of Caleb's real father's name.

"We have to read all of Claire's letters. It's safe to assume Chloe didn't know about the pregnancy since it's never mentioned."

Both men professed their love for Claire. Lunch forgotten, one by one, she read the letters and relayed the shortened version to Blake. When Sarah came to the last letter her hand shook. The energy swirling around the room had intensified and she was positive this letter would hold the answers.

My darling,

I am pleased to hear of our impending child. I know the circumstances are not great, but you know my love for you is greater than all things. You must come to stay at my apartment whilst I am gone. I must leave shortly and report for duty. I shall return before the baby is born and we can be married. Enclosed is a key to my place. Hopefully, I will receive a promotion and that will help me to provide for you in a fitting manner. My heart is forever yours. Come to me, my darling. Forever.
Yours, Jack

Tears fell down Sarah's face. It was a love like all who believed in love searched for. It was a love like she wanted. And it was for that love, Claire had thrown away everything good in her life to go for something greater. She'd risked everything for love. They didn't find out why Jack Spry never returned. Another love story with a heartbreaking ending—the worst kind. But perhaps another mystery to be solved one day.

In its place however, a new love story had begun. She and Blake were not related and any mental hang-up she had no longer mattered. The sense of relief she felt was more than enough to convince her she wouldn't have been able to walk away completely no matter what they found out. The rest, however, was up to them to discover if they were bound for a great love story with a happy ending.

Blake hadn't said a word.

"We have our answer. It would appear Caleb is the son of Claire and Jack. And Blake, please believe me, I'm sorry I ever had a second's hesitation."

Sarah stepped in close letting her hand fall to his chest, the familiar warmth filling her.

"Are you sure? It appears Caleb is Jack's son, but it's not definite. There's always the possibility she'd slept with the captain and was going to marry Jack. Women have done such things in the past and I'm sure it will continue to happen in the future. I don't want us to move forward unless you're sure."

Why was he casting a shadow of doubt?

Assurance.

"I'm sure. And we can skip the DNA test because it doesn't matter. Unless, of course, you decide to trace your family history further. But either way, I'm okay with the answer because I think this is our turn for a love story."

Blake pulled her into his arms and kissed her. It felt like coming home. She'd been crazy to think she could resist this but felt blessed to have been pointed in the right direction.

Thank you, Chloe.

Time would tell where things would go with Blake, but at least she wouldn't be standing in the way of her own happiness. In the meantime, Sarah had her work cut out. Between the letters and the journal, she was more than armed and ready to take on the military court system and apply for the restoration of Captain Tremont's honor. Not to mentioned armed with plenty of material for her next story—one that had all the makings of a best seller.

***

Chloe smiled. Captain Tremont would have his day in court and the truth would set her free. As for her sister, she was sorry for the tragic ending of her life. It didn't matter that Claire had been the spoiled one, always seeking the limelight and acting out after their mother died. Chloe had been the stronger of the two and she'd taken her twin under her wing and protected her.

And whatever Claire wanted, she got. Including Jack and the captain. Two men who loved her completely hardly seemed fair. It hadn't mattered that Chloe herself had fallen in love at first sight with the handsome captain, or that at one point, she could have sworn the captain had his eye on her.

But she couldn't compete with Claire's charm and once she'd staked her claim, there was no turning back. Instead, Chloe had resigned herself to be the wallflower.

It had been a secret love triangle no one knew had existed, least of all her sister and the captain. But Sarah and Blake were another story. Chloe had no doubt their love would survive and flourish because there was nothing one-sided about what they felt for each other. Chloe sighed in satisfaction as she watched the young couple.

Epilogue

SIX MONTHS LATER...

Sarah was ten long minutes away from Blake's house. She couldn't wait to see him again and share all her good news. Normally, they were together during the weekends to work on remodeling the new house he bought, but for the past two weeks she'd been unable to head to Cedar Grove.

It hadn't taken Blake long after the discovery of the Westerly painting to buy the old homestead when it came up for sale. It was almost as if it were his destiny.

She'd been more than a little surprised to discover her construction abilities and basked in the glow of a job well done with each completed project. The same we she felt when she finished a story. The same way she felt when her new novel, The Ghost and Captain Tremont, was accepted for publication. And the same when she felt when the letter from the courthouse arrived today.

She slid out of the car and headed up the walkway a quick clip, taking the steps like she was dancing on air.

Blake greeted her at the top step, his arms coming around her to pull her close. His zest for life shown in everything he did, and it was just one of the reasons she'd fallen in love with him.

"Hey, beautiful." He murmured the greeting right before he claimed her mouth in a welcome kiss.

"Hey, you." She pulled away to look at him, fighting back the happy tears that came to the surface.

"What gives? Did you win the lottery or something?" He chuckled.

"Or something." She waved the envelope in the air. "I got it. I got the letter from the military court. They've exonerated Captain Tremont of all smuggling charges and have changed his records to reflect an honorable discharge."

"Congratulations. You lobbied hard for this and your efforts paid off." He pulled her into his arms rewarding her with another of his heartwarming kisses.

"Wait. It gets better. They're holding a ceremonial burial for him at the Arlington National Cemetery, one befitting the late Honorable Captain John Tremont."

"That is wonderful news."

"And there's more." She grinned.

"More? It's only been two weeks since I've seen you and two days since we talked." Blake grinned.

"Well, this part I found out last week but wanted to tell you when I got here. My story went under contract. The publisher loves Captain Tremont's story and get this, they want me to write another one. Make it a series."

"I knew it would happen. This is cause for celebration. And I know the perfect way to start it off." Blake's answering smile grew wide, his expression suddenly one of determination. He dropped his arms and stepped back, reaching into his pocket.

Sarah cocked her head to one side, her eyes opening wide when she spotted the black box in his hand. Her heart raced triple time, the meaning of the moment fully hitting her.

Dropping to one knee, he took her hand in his. "Sarah Marie Dalton, I love you. I want you by my side every day, sharing our journey through life and whatever it may bring. Will you do me the honor of marrying me?"

Her hand covered her heart as she inhaled sharply. "Oh, my gosh." Tears filled her eyes and ran down her face, even as she tried to brush them away. She wrapped her arms around his neck, flashing him the most beautiful smile she could muster. "Why, yes, Sir Carter, I do believe I shall marry you. For you see, I love you, too." Sarah kissed him, the joy in her heart overflowing. Blake had been worth taking a chance with her heart. This time the love was real and forever.

He slid the ring on her finger.

"It's beautiful."

"A beautiful ring for a beautiful woman." Blake stood and kissed her, the love in his heart written in the reverence of his eyes as he gazed down at her.

"By the way, our home is finished and ready for you to move in as soon as you marry me."

"I never figured you'd be a complete stickler for the rules of convention, but I love that about you."

"You heard what Father Monroe told me when we were researching those files. And since you've already got me going to church on Sundays, I wouldn't want to go up against Father Monroe, or I might be forced to go to confession as well." He laughed.

"Then I suggest we make a beeline to share the good news with Jason. I know it's Friday night, but I wonder if you can get us a reservation?"

"No worries. I already made one for tonight, because I was planning on proposing to you at dinner. But the timing is better now." He leaned forward and kissed her again.

"I agree. Jason will lose a regular customer after we're married, but I'm sure he'll be happy for us. Especially considering he's just one of many who thought they had us all figured out a long time ago."

"Turns out they were right." He winked.

They arrived at the Crestfield Inn a few minutes before seven. Jason greeted them at the entrance to the Garden Delight Café. "It's nice to see you two again." The two men shook hands, Jason reserving his hug for Sarah.

"Thanks. It's only been a couple of weeks." She shook her head and grinned.

"True. Have you checked in yet?"

"No, I'll do it after dinner."

"We've got a full house, but I reserved the best table I could for you. It's too cold this time of year to put you outside. You owe me one, Sarah, because believe me, Blake tried to talk me into it."

Sarah glance at Blake and then down her left ring finger. His special night started early, but she loved the boyish excitement he exuded when something mattered to him. And she mattered. It was the best feeling in the world.

They followed Jason across the room toward back of the room to a cozy corner table.

"When you have a second, we've got something to tell you." Sarah was bursting with excitement and the need share their good news.

"Don't keep me in suspense. Talk while I open your wine." Jason chuckled.

"Sarah's agreed to marry me," Blake said, a wide smile on his face.

"Congratulations! In that case, dinner is on me. Wonderful news." Jason shook Blake's hand. "I was wondering when it was going to happen. Actually, I suspected it might be tonight."

"He had planned on it, but things got a little crazy before we got here." Sarah held out her hand for inspection.

"It would seem Blake has good choice in women and in jewelry." Jason grinned.

"And there's more." Sarah reached into her purse and pulled out the envelope. "I got a letter from the courts, and they reversed all the charges against Captain Tremont." Excitedly, she filled Jason in with the important deals to catch him up to speed. "Wow. You guys are full of great news. I wish I could stop and celebrate with you but..." Jason waved his hand to indicate all the other tables filled with guests. "When's the wedding?"

"That's what we wanted to talk to you about. We were hoping we could have a small wedding here—before Christmas. This old-fashioned guy has been listening to Father Monroe and won't let me move in unless we're married. It'll be easier if I don't have to keep traveling this road and taking the ferry through the winter." Sarah winked at Jason, but this time he didn't have the same sense of jealousy. He was confident in her love and the knowledge they would be together for life.

"Is that the only reason you want to marry me so soon?" Blake teased.

"Well, there's that, and then there's you." Their eyes met and held as Blake reached for her hand. Soulmates.

"That's my exit to leave. And yes, we will put together whatever you need for a wedding. Again, congratulations to you both." Jason wandered off, stopping at several tables to greet a couple of new arrivals.

***

Chloe danced and twirled with joy. She'd sensed Sarah and Blake's presence the minute they'd entered the inn. She hovered nearby, always anxious for the latest information and updates.

Tonight, the news provided a doubly delicious moment.

Captain Tremont's honor had been restored and Sarah and Blake were engaged.

Chloe's work was done.

The look of love between the happy couple warmed her soul and filled her with content. After they left, she realized it would soon be time for her to leave. The thought didn't bring her the satisfaction she expected. Instead, a feeling of sadness washed over her, and she realized she didn't want to leave.

This place was her home, and it was the place she'd been the happiest in her life, even if only for the space of one dance. She might not have been able to find true love for herself, but for those who can't—you help others to do. Playing matchmaker for Sarah and Blake had brought her an unexpected joy. Chloe returned to her room and looked around. She moved to the window, never growing tired of the view of the gardens. This time, however, a light glowed in the distance. The glow grew larger and brighter and came closer.

Mesmerized, she couldn't turn away. Suddenly she understood. It was time to make her decision. The light was for her. Did she leave, or did she stay?

To her surprise, a lone figure came forth from the light and walked toward her. It couldn't be. It wasn't possible. She closed her eyes and checked again. Nothing changed.

Captain Tremont.

He smiled, one much like the smile he bestowed upon her once upon a time. Her heart melted all over again. Dashing in his naval uniform, the man she'd always loved stood before her, holding out his hand, beckoning her to join him. She placed her hand in his and watched him bow.

"I'm sorry, Chloe. I know there's nothing I can do to correct the wrong, but please, know in my heart, I'm sorry."

He was speaking to her—but she was a ghost. Ghost weren't visited by ghosts—were they?

"Why are you here?" It was the only thing she could think to say.

"To tell you I'm sorry and to tell you thanks. But also, to see if you..."

"What?" Chloe knew this couldn't be real. Her mind was playing tricks with her.

"To see if you and I, if you might consider giving me a second chance."

She felt something strange in the vicinity of her heart—a warmth she couldn't ignore. What did he mean a second chance, ghosts couldn't fall in love—could they?"

"I don't understand. There's no reason on earth for you to say these things. I was the one who sent you the note and it's me who is sorry. I should have minded my own business. I've never forgiven myself for what happened to you that night and beg your forgiveness."

"*We have all made mistakes along the way. And now, we've been freed from them.*"

"*Yes, you are free to leave. Honorably, you know.*" *She smiled at him.* "*Sarah's your great-granddaughter many moons forward, but she discovered the truth and righted the wrong the military did to you.*"

"*I know. And you, my dear, are also free to leave. You didn't need to stay on my account, but I'm glad you did. Shall we leave together?*" *Once again, he held out his hand.*

She raised her hand but stopped midway. For so long she'd dreamt of this moment, but now that it was here, it was too late. She couldn't believe what she was about to do, but it was the right decision. For her. "*No.*"

"*What do you mean?*" *The captain looked taken aback.*

She didn't expect him to understand, and maybe she was a fool to stay, but matchmaking gave her a purpose. It made her happy. And she didn't want to always wonder if she was the captain's second choice, her sister out of his reach.

"I choose to stay. I like it here and I enjoy helping others find love. It gives me a joy I never knew in life." She backed away from the captain, trying hard to resist the temptation he offered.

"Do you still love me?" A loaded question, but one that changed nothing.

"Of course. But you love Claire, and spending eternity watching you pine for her is not what I choose."

"That's where you're wrong. There's something you need to know before you cast me away. When I first met you and your sister, it was you who captured my attention. I was drawn to your gentle spirit and inner strength. After our dance, I was afraid to approach you too quickly for fear of disgracing you in front of the others. I danced with several others that evening before I could return and ask you to dance again.

When you turned me down, I decided I'd misread your interest. Your sister seemed far keener on pursuing a relationship. The truth is, I needed a mother for my infant daughter, and I was looking for a wife. Had I not misread your response,

I would not have been willing to settle for your lookalike."

Nothing could have shocked her more. Chloe played out the evening in her head and realized his explanation was entirely possible. It was Claire who'd pronounced her interest and staked her claim on the captain and having always given in to her sister, it never occurred to Chloe to fight for what she wanted.

"Thank you for telling me that. I'm sorry I gave you the wrong impression, but my sister had already danced with you and laid claim. I made it a habit to never show interest in a man she'd chosen first. We were twins and it would never have a good outcome."

He shook his head. "So many years that could have been different."

"You best hurry, Captain. The light is fading. Your window to leave is closing."

The captain turned to face the light. He took a step forward and stopped.

He turned back. "No. My light is standing in front of me. I choose to stay with you this time. I know how I felt when I first saw you, and I was right. Only a woman of character and one deeply in love would have spent hundreds of years trying to restore my honor for something that wasn't her fault. There's no greater love than that. I can't change the past, but I can change the future. I choose to stay with you. It may have taken me two hundred years to figure all this out, but I have, and if you're staying, I'm staying right here with you—where I belong."

Chloe moved to stand close, his arms coming around her. The warmth filled her heart and seeped into her soul. "Are you sure? You don't have to do this."

"I'm sure. Besides, I wouldn't want to miss my own funeral." He chuckled. The music started, and the captain stepped back, one hand at her waist, the other holding her arm out as he led her around the bedroom floor for their second dance. He twirled her around and pulled her close—the two of them moving as one.

For eternity.

What to read next...
She doesn't trust easily. He needs a miracle. Will a delightful supermarket dalliance grant the floral fragrance of happily ever after? Pick up a copy of
T
urning Up Roses
to find out...
 Recovering from an injury, the last thing she needs is the media limelight. Or a handsome avalanche flattening her on the ski slopes. Pick up a copy of ***Turning Down Pie*** to find out what happens...

***

If you enjoyed this sweet and charming romance, be sure to check out the ALSO BY ELSIE DAVIS section on the next page for more clean and wholesome romance.

BONUS READ

Want to keep in touch with new releases and what's happening in the world of Elsie Davis?

Sign up for the monthly newsletter at (https://www.elsiedavishea.com) Elsie Davis HEA (Happily-Ever-After) and enjoy DIG-GING THE DRIVER (A Celebrity Corgi Ro-mance) as a FREE BOOK!

The greatest compliment you could give an author is to leave a review in order to help other readers discover the same great stories you enjoyed. Amazon/Book-bub/Goodreads are all great places. Many thanks!!!

Another great way to keep in touch - ***Follow Elsie Davis on FaceBook***

For more sweet, clean, and wholesome Happily-Ever-After Sweet Romances, be sure to check out ALSO BY ELSIE DAVIS.

And if you love Christian Inspirational ro-mance, be sure to check out CROSSROADS

CREEK COWBOYS! Cowboys down on their luck, love, and laughter, who get a second chance at happiness.

The greatest compliment you could give an author is to leave a review in order to help other readers discover the same great stories you enjoyed. Amazon/Bookbub/Goodreads are all great places. Many thanks!!!

Want to keep in touch with new releases and what's happening in the world of Elsie Davis? ***Sign up for the monthly newsletter here... Elsie Davis HEA (Happily-Ever-After)*** **And while you're there, be sure to check out the new Elsie Davis Bookstore where you can purchase books directly at a discounted price.**

Another great way to keep in touch - ***Follow Elsie Davis on FaceBook***

Also By Elsie Davis

Sweet, Clean and Wholesome Stories...with a Happily-Ever-After Guarantee!

Holidays in Hallbrook
(Sweet Romance Series for Holidays Throughout the Year)
Welcome to Hallbrook, New Hampshire. A small-town filled with the unexpected, lots of love, and of course, a beloved dog to ramp up the excitement.
Love & Order (Labor Day)
Love & Family (Thanksgiving)
Love & Peace (Christmas)
Love & Chocolate (Valentine's Day)
Love & Hope (Mother's Day)

Love & Liberty (Independence Day)
Love & Honor (Veteran's Day)
Love & Joy (Easter)
Love & Adventure (Father's Day)

Great Smoky Mountain Getaways
(Christian Inspirational – Women's Fiction Romances)
Juliet's Journey to Love
Poppy's Path to Love
Rachel's Road to Love

Crossroads Creek Cowboys
(Christian Inspirational Romances)
The Heart of a Cowboy
The Help of a Cowboy
The Return of a Cowboy
Coming Soon – The Care of a Cowboy

Crestfield Inn Romances

If you like special kinds of soulmates, a splash of the supernatural, and wholesome relationships, you'll adore this sweet bit of fun filled with romance and mystery.

Turning Back Time
Turning Up Roses
Turning Down Pie

Celebrity Corgi Romance
(Standalone Sweet Romance)

If you like light mystery mixed in with your happily-ever-after, you'll enjoy this second-chance romance and the race to save an adorable Corgi.

Digging the Driver

Gold Coast Retrievers
(Sweet Romance)

Special Golden Retrievers help their humans solve mysteries, save lives, and even find love...

Defending Dakota

Trinity River
(Sweet Western Romance)
Ranchers and farmers depend on the Trinity River for water, but when a secret conglomerate starts buying up property by fair means or foul, it's time for the landowners of Tumble County to fight back—Texas style. But what they don't count on, is finding love in the process.
Back in the Rancher's Arms
Small Town, Big Secrets

Coming Soon! (2023-2024)

Sundancer's Legacy – 9 Book series

Sundancer's Star
Sundancer's Joy

Sundancer's Heart
Sundancer's Majesty
Sundancer's Miracle
Sundancer's Glory
Sundancer's Kiss
Sundancer's Moon
Sundancer's Splendor

About The Author

Elsie Davis is a *USA Today and International Bestselling Author* of over 25 sweet, clean, and wholesome romances, and a member of the ACFW. She discovered the world of Happily-Ever-After romance at the age of twelve when she began avidly reading Barbara Cartland, the Queen of Romance, and has been hooked ever since. After building her dream log home on top of a small mountain, she turned her attention to do what she loves most, writing. Elsie writes sweet Contemporary Romance and Contemporary Christian Romance from her heart...hoping to share a little love in a big world.

When she's not writing, she can be found birding, kayaking, camping, fishing, playing disc golf, and taking nature walks—hoping to spot wildlife. Basically, she loves all things outdoors, EXCEPT cold weather. She and her husband are avid Caribbean cruisers, but Elsie's favorite vacation was their cruise to Alaska. (In spite of the cold!) Indoors, she enjoys a toasty fire, and of course, a great romance with a guaranteed Happily-Ever-After.

https://www.elsiedavishea.com